FIRE AND CINDER

BOOK 6 OF THE FAIRY TALES OF THE MAGICORUM

CHRISTINA BAUER

COPYRIGHT

Newton, MA 02464
www.monsterhousebooks.com
ISBN 9781946677600

DEDICATION

For All Those Who Kick Ass, Take Names, and Read Books

CONTENTS

ALSO BY CHRISTINA BAUER

STANDARD APPENDIX OF COOL STUFF

EXTRA APPENDIX THAT TAKES THE FIRST ONE AND KICKS ITS ASS

COLLECTED WORKS

Fairy Tales of the Magicorum

Modern fairy tales with sass, action, and romance

1. Wolves and Roses
2. Moonlight and Midtown
3. Shifters and Glyphs
4. Slippers and Thieves
5. Bandits and Ball Gowns
6. Fire and Cinder
7. Fairies and Frosting
8. Towers and Tithes
9. Evil Queens and Goblin Kings

Angelbound Origins

About a quasi (part demon and part human) girl who loves kicking butt in Purgatory's Arena

1. Angelbound
2. Scala
3. Acca
4. Thrax

Angelbound Xavier

Xavier's story

1. Archenemy
2. Archnemesis
3. Archangel

Pixieland Diaries

Sassy pixie Calla loves elf prince Dare. Too bad he hasn't noticed her. Yet.

1. Pixieland Diaries
2. Calla
3. Dare
4. Winter Prince
5. Ley Queen

Dimension Drift

Dystopian adventures with science, snark, and hot aliens

1. Scythe
2. Umbra
3. Alien Minds
4. ECHO Academy

*This is a completed series.

Beholder

Where a medieval farm girl discovers necromancy and true love

1. Cursed
2. Concealed
3. Cherished
4. Crowned
5. Cradled

*This is a completed series.

FIRE AND CINDER

ELLE

I sprawl back-first onto the couch and unbutton the top of my jeans. The reason? My stomach is over-stuffed with deep-dish pizza and gross self-pity.

Welcome to the *new normal* at Chez Elle.

All around, the floor is littered with take-out boxes and unopened mail. There's a postcard which reads, *congratulations on finishing high school online.* I use it as a napkin.

None of this sloth-like existence is my fault. *Mostly.* My life sucks lately because an evil elf named Nal'Adel chucked my boyfriend, Alec, into a magical prison. I tried a rescue attempt, failed, and have been moping around ever since.

Which may be my fault *a little*. It's not like I'm tied to the couch. But if I eat all the things, I find I can avoid facing any renegade sense of responsibility. So far, it's been working like a charm.

Leaning over, I scoop an old take-out cup from the floor and check the contents. *Huh. Looks like a green milkshake. But is the flavor mint or week-old mold? Hard to tell.* I set the container aside. Some stuff is best left a mystery.

If only my roomie, Bry, were here. She'd slob-shame me into cleaning up. But Bry is off on an adventure. Without her, I'm like a human marble trapped in the empty shoebox of my apartment, rolling around without path or purpose. For now, I've temporarily landed in the living room.

Closing my eyes, I picture what I should be doing at this moment: *rescuing Alec.* I've done some snooping around. Life in an enchanted prison is no picnic. Alec could be making knives out of garbage and fighting for a decent place to hide. Just thinking about it makes me want to barf and-or scream.

Which is why I have his entire rescue planned out. Like a warrior queen of old, I would leave the familiar streets of Manhattan and take off for the dangerous Realm of Faerie. All the while, I'd yell my words of vengeance…

"Behold," I would shout. "For I am on a mission to free Alec and punish his jailer, Nal'Adel!"

Anyway, that's the ideal version of my life. In reality, I already tried to open a portal into Faerie… but chickened out before ever reaching Nal'Adel. In my defense, there were lots of doors involved and no clear way to get bio breaks. After forty-eight hours, I lost my nerve and came home.

Hauling my ass off the couch, I slog over to my bedroom. Most of my life is pretty bizarre, so I decorated this place in a look I like to call, *generic eighteen year old.* There are white walls, pink pillows, and a few stuffed animals. These days, it's what happens *outside* my apartment building that's unusual.

Plunking down at my desk, I scan through my hi-rise window and inspect the sidewalk far below. *Any enchanted humans out there?* For some reason, a team of magical stalkers have been following me around lately. These folks are hard to miss, what with their large signs and tendency to shout my name.

But no one is lurking today. *Boo.* Disappointment twists within me. Is it sick that I'm so desperate for company, I look forward to my daily dose of enspelled humanity? Definitely. Because the real problem is how I truly miss one person.

Alec.

Memories appear. I'll never forget the first time I stole gems from Alec's office at Le Charme Jewelers. Okay, I know this isn't typical romance stuff, but my life is pretty much a shit show. I'll take what I can get.

Back then, I was repossessing a vampire's tiara from Alec's desk when I found a picture of the boy himself. Since he's a celebrity, most photos of Alec are pretty staged. Not this one. It showed Alec playing with puppies in Central Park. The guy looked so joyful, handsome and fun. Simply put, my ovaries melted.

After that caper, I'd make a point to check Alec's office for new photos any time I stopped by to un-steal more jewels. One or two selfies were always waiting for me on his desk. What I didn't know was that the extra images weren't a coincidence. Alec had been watching replays of my crimes from his security camera feeds. He was purposefully leaving behind new pics for me to enjoy.

It was love at first felony.

Eventually, I went to the Glass Slipper Ball, almost got myself killed, and found out that Alec and I cared for each other. Now he's trapped inside an enchanted gemstone. Meanwhile, I'm eating my feelings while honing my anti-social skills.

The moment freezes. I catch my reflection on my

windowpane. I resemble a classic Cinderella, what with my blue eyes and blonde hair. That said, the smeared mascara and questionable food stain on my chin are new additions to my regular fairy tale look. Three words come to mind.

This. Isn't. Me.

For the first time in ages, anger zings through my nervous system. Something inside my soul snaps. Rising, I pace my bedroom and give myself a little motivational speech.

Is talking to myself a cool thing to do? *No.*

Therapy-worthy? *Probably.*

Necessary? *Fuck, yeah.*

"Come on," I begin. "I'm Magicorum. That means fate has always tried forcing me into the fairy tale template for Cinderella. But did I serve a pack of psychos while singing to rodents? No way. I got off my butt, un-stole some jewels, and escaped my evil stepfamily."

Which is true. At that happy thought, I straighten my stance. Hell, I even brush some cookie crumbs off my jeans. Pep Talk Time is totally helping, so I keep right on going.

"And that's just for starters," I announce. "All Magicorum are shifters, witches or fae. I'm a fairy who's lousy with power. Sure, I really don't know dick about spell casting. Yet, did I allow lack-o-knowledge to stop me from un-stealing my first brooch? Nuh uh. And I shouldn't let it block me from opening portals, either."

I nod once, the decision made. *No more sitting around. It's beyond time to reopen the portal... and walk through it forever, if that's what it takes to reach Faerie.*

ELLE

*N*ow that I've decided to leave, the apartment becomes eerily still around me. An expectant kind of energy charges the air. It's as if every corner is screaming, *don't forget! Bry will return.*

A question appears. What will happen when my roomie comes back and finds the place empty?

Nothing good, I'm sure.

When I first took off for Faerie, I rushed away without leaving a note behind. Not cool. I must record a message before my next disappearing act. Hey, it's the least I can do. So I re-park my butt at my desk, flick on my laptop, and start a video.

"Hey, Bry." I nibble my bottom lip and debate what to say next. *How do I explain all the awful things that have gone down?*

An idea appears. There are two more greetings to go through before getting to the nasty stuff. *Yay, procrastination!*

"Hi, Knox." That's Bry's boyfriend.

For my final hello, I add in a little wave. Because this one's really important.

"And greetings to you, oh Colonel Mallory the Magnificent." He's a powerful fae and dragon shifter. The Colonel also happens to be the guy who's leading my roomie's adventure away from home.

Months ago, Bry, Knox, Alec, and I released tons of magic. Afterward, the world should've become lousy with power. That's not what happened. If anything, magic kept fading. So the Colonel took Bry and Knox on a quest to figure out what's up. I don't know where they are, what they're doing, or when they'll return. All of which makes it a classic Colonel Mallory operation.

"Hope you're having a great time." I force a smile. Major fail. Turns out, there's nothing more lonely than pretend-talking to your non-existent friends. "You're probably wondering why Alec isn't here with me. Everyone knows he can't resist a good video bomb."

Now for the tough part.

"It's like this." I hold up a tabloid from last year. The headline reads, *Alec Le Charme Drinks Coffee—Just Like Us!* "This is classic Alec." I set the tabloid down. "You also know how he got stuck running Le Charme." Next I raise a glossy magazine toward the camera which reads, *Alec Le Charme... Hottest CEO Or Hottest CEO Ever?*

The cover shot makes my stomach go fluttery. My boyfriend is the perfect mash-up of surfer boy casual and male model fashionista... all with a knee-melting smile.

Damn, do I ever miss him.

"And here's what happened after you left." I lift a final newspaper with the headline, *Alec Le Charme Is Dead.*

I quickly toss the gloomy thing aside. "I'm guessing you haven't seen this news yet. Because if you did, then you'd definitely be in touch. And honestly? I'm a little worried about the radio silence from you guys." I force another grin. "Yet you're probably fine. Bry and Knox are werewolves for crying out loud. And Colonel Mallory is a badass dragon shifter. Chances are, you three are just busy tracking down all that missing magic."

Leaning forward, I brace myself for the big reveal. "Here's the situation. Alec isn't dead. An evil elf named Nal'Adel imprisoned him inside a magical gemstone. Strange, right?"

In my mind, I picture them all agreeing with me by saying things like, *Odd stuff, Elle!* My imaginary version of Bry even gives me a hug. It helps.

"By now, you can probably guess the deal. I'm not in the apartment. Alec is imprisoned in Faerie. Clearly, I've gone after him. So you know, this will be my second rescue attempt. In the first one, I got freaked out because my transport spell opened too many doors. But I've read a lot about magic since that fail."

Which is true. It's amazing what you can discover when you have the internet and extra time on your hands.

"Here's what I've learned." I tap my temple for emphasis. "What I lack in casting know-how, I can make up for in terms of raw power. For my next spell, I'll just pump in tons of magic and strong-arm the thing into working. Boom!"

I slump back on my chair. That sounds like a logical idea, but it could totally backfire. After I opened my first portal, I spent two days roaming through magical doors and got myself seriously dehydrated. In the end, it was touch-and-go. I wasn't even sure I could cast a spell to get home. Yet since that disaster, I've come up with a new scheme.

Even so, what if this new plan is worse than the last one?

My thoughts run through my options once more. There's always the possibility to find outside help. Sadly, my attempts to contact friends—namely Knox, Bry, Jacoby and Colonel Mallory—have failed. There are other Magicorum kids at my old school, but they're just learning how to boil water with their powers. It's not like any of them could do much. And my teachers freaked out when my enchanted humans showed up to class. Announcing that I'm about to single-handedly invade Faerie won't go over well.

Moving on.

I have black market contacts, but none of them will talk to me. They're just as twitchy about the enspelled stalkers as everyone at school.

In the end, it doesn't matter how I look at it, my best option is to cast big and hope for the best. If things do go wrong, at least my friends will know where to look for me.

Anyway, that's my plan and I'm sticking to it.

I refocus on the camera. "Now you know everything." I exhale a long breath. "Wish me luck."

Reaching forward, I move to exit the video app. Then I pause. These might be the final words my friends ever hear from me.

"I love you guys," I say quietly.

And I click off the vid feed.

Time to make some magic.

3

ELLE

*I*t's a habit to check my appearance before going anywhere major. The Realm of Faerie is no exception. So I scan my reflection in my bedroom mirror. Who knows what they wear in Faerie? My jeans and sweater combo should be fine. I wipe the food stain off my chin, run a brush through my hair, and VOILA. I'm ready to take on an evil elf.

Now to test my theory. If I force extra power into my spell, will that make it work?

Reaching into my soul, I sense the magic that always churns within me. Last time, I politely called upon that power by thinking encouraging thoughts. Now, I decide to yell out orders.

"Get moving!"

Fairy dust pours from my palms. The sparkling bits whirl through the air before whipping across the room and soaking into the far wall. The entire chamber pulses with magic.

"Make me a portal."

The barest outline of a door appears in the far wall. Not

great. Better shove more energy into this casting. With all my focus, I call upon my inner reserves of magic.

"Come on! Move it!"

Heavier cords of pink fairy dust shoot from my palms and slam into the far wall. Furniture wobbles. Books tumble. Shelves collapse. My stuffed unicorn explodes.

I smile my face off. *This is working.*

A spiderweb of cracks appear on the opposite panel. Light fixtures shatter in the ceiling, sending glass cascading onto the floor. An ethereal wind whips through my collection of take-out boxes.

Then my entire back wall explodes.

Where once there were plasterboard panels and a few unicorn pictures, now there's an open field complete with grass, shrubs and a setting sun.

My eyes widen. An indoor vista? That's different from last time. I approach the not-a-wall. Reaching out, I touch what feels to be a glass panel. It sits right where my wall used to be, and it separates me from the greenery beyond.

A warm sense of satisfaction spreads through my chest. *I am totally nailing this magic thing.*

Flashes of pink light appear in the center of the clear wall. When the brightness dies down, there's a new addition to my room…

An emerald-colored door now sits in the middle of the fake landscape.

Alec, here I come!

I pull on the handle. It opens with ease. Once I cross the threshold, the door snaps shut at my back. I'm trapped in a two-foot-wide space with nothing but white walls for company. Pink magic glimmers in the air. Another door appears before me.

My stomach sinks. This is just like last time. Wincing, I open the second door. Then I smile my face off.

Yay, an actual space!

Sure, what I'm looking at isn't a traditional place—it's more a bunch of smoke and strangeness, but why be picky? This is a huge improvement. With any luck, Alec or Nal'Adel will be hidden in this fog. Adrenaline spikes through my bloodstream.

With cautious steps, I shuffle through the smoke. Chilly mist settles on my skin. The scent of dust and mold fills the air. Floorboards creak with my every step. That gets me thinking. Squeaky wood means that I'm in a room, not a garden. *Good to know.*

Little by little, I move deeper into the mist. The hair on my neck stands on end. No doubt about it. Someone else is in here.

That's when I see the truth—a tall figure lurks within the shadows. My breath catches.

Is it Alec? Nal'Adel?

The mists slowly lessen. Soon, I can make out the scene before me with perfect clarity.

And Alec isn't here at all. Neither is Nal'Adel.

It's my mother, Rae, and she's holding a baby version of me.

What the WHAT?

ELLE'S DOOR

4

ELLE

*N*ow that the smoke is gone, it looks like I stand inside an old timey version of Cynder Mercantile, the family business-n-homestead where I grew up. Plus, there's a matching incarnation of Mom and Baby Me.

That settles it.

I'm having some kind of magic-induced illusion. There's no way I am actually strolling through history.

But if it *is* a fake vision, then why does everything seem so real? The place appears just as I remember, from the cinderblock walls to the slatted wood floor. The air even holds that familiar scent of dust and mold particular to Cynder Mercantile.

Crap. This is totally happening.

Anger tightens across my neck and shoulders. Damn, this spell misfired… and now it's sidelining my rescue of Alec. I run through what I learned about magical prisons. Alec is safe. Maybe. He's not hungry. Possibly.

Gah, this isn't really helping. Now that I've started my quest to free Alec, doing anything else feels like torture.

Then my gaze locks onto my mother, Rae. She died so young; I can't remember the last time I saw her whole and healthy. After Mom's burial, my stepmother, Marchesa, destroyed all the pictures of Rae that she could find. Over the years, I even forgot what my own mother looked like.

For a moment, all my worries fade into the background as I soak in the sight of Rae Cynder. She is the epitome of her first name. Mom's hair shines like golden beams of light, her eyes are sky-blue, and she radiates a sunny disposition without saying a word.

Bands of sorrow tighten around my chest. Mom slowly lost her luster over years of illness. I haven't seen her like this —all lively and bright—since I was eleven years old. On her deathbed, Mom insisted that Dad marry Marchesa, my eventual stepmother and nemesis. Sadly, my birth parents always followed the classic Cinderella fairy tale template.

But the vision before me now? It takes place years before that tragedy began. This Rae holds a fat Baby Me on her hip while marching around the empty warehouse that would soon become Cynder Mercantile.

"What do you think?" Mom asks Baby Me. "Should we set up our shop here?"

On reflex, I call out a reply. "Yes, this place is perfect!" My breath catches as I wait to see if Mom notices my grown-up self.

She doesn't.

Which isn't a shock. It's hard enough to summon magic that helps you see the past, let alone interact with it. And it's not like I meant to cast this particular spell in the first place. I just pumped a ton of energy into my portal and this is the result.

Guess I got a little carried away. *Oops.*

Mom bounces Baby Me on her hip. "This particular area could be used for storing things. We might place the artisans on the level above. There's another great spot where we'd live together as a family." She steps around in a slow circle. "Oh, this could definitely work."

I hug my elbows. My parents created Cynder Mercantile. The business allowed enchanted artisans to make beautiful things that we sold in our storefront.

At this point, I can't help but compare my parents' great achievement with my own less-than-awesome life. I un-steal jewelry that someone else took first... which I then return to the rightful owner. The ethics of it aren't perfect, but un-stealing has paid the bills and kept me free from my evil step-family. Even so, I can't imagine building up something like Cynder Mercantile with anyone else.

Not even Alec.

My boyfriend is already the CEO of Le Charme Jewelers, one of the largest retail chains in the world. Even if Alec and I get through all this stuff with Nal'Adel, how could I join in on something like Le Charme? I'm not exactly your typical Cinderella.

Much as I hate to admit this, my love of thievery fits a lot more into the story of Aladdin than anything else.

At least, that's what the genie, Skye, keeps telling me.

Across the room, Mom keeps talking to Baby Me about all her plans for Cynder Mercantile. My parents were always so solid on their life path.

It's never been that way for me.

I rub my neck and think things through. Maybe Skye is right—I should become an Aladdin-style genie. That would mean swearing off relationships and turning into a major kook, but at least I'd be a happy type of nut job. Isn't that what's most important anyway?

Suddenly, a shower of sparkling white particles appear across the darkened warehouse. *Fairy magic.* A new figure materializes from the glimmering curtain. Seeing the face, my skin chills over with shock.

"Is that you, Nal'Adel?" I ask.

The elf doesn't answer. Just like with Mom, the newcomer can't detect that I'm here. I step nearer. Maybe it's just someone who looks a lot like the bitch that jammed my boyfriend into a magical prison. In reality, I could be looking at Nal'Adel's cousin or something.

Up close, it's clear that this mystery lady is hiding her pointy ears under a glamour spell. She also sports a slightly different dress than usual. But her big hair and judgy face are unmistakable.

This is the real deal. Nal'Adel is in the building.

I fight the urge to groan. Isn't portaling to my own past bad enough? Why does Nal'Adel have to spell-bomb my life right now? What's she really doing here anyway?

As if to answer my many questions, Mom turns to Nal'Adel and smiles. "Hello, fairy godmother."

This time, I don't hold back my groan.

NAL'ADEL

5

ELLE

Nal'Adel is here? Time for a mental regroup.

My mother lived by a Cinderella life template, the same as I (sort of) do. And based on what I see now, Nal'Adel acted as the fairy godmother to my mom, Rae Cynder.

As revelations go, this isn't great. My head turns cloudy with worry. I don't think I can handle much more drama. Not to mention the fact that the pizza I ate for breakfast has started doing the cha-cha on my small intestines.

Nal'Adel sighs. "I remember your ball as if it were yesterday."

Mom winks. "As I recall, it was a dance to celebrate the Queen of the County Fair. That's hardly a royal ball."

"It counts for your fairy tale life template," states Nal'Adel. "Both you and Marchesa were competing for the title of Queen. And Declan chose you."

A wistful look shines in Mom's blue eyes. "That he did."

"And now you and Declan have a baby." Nal'Adel flit-walks closer to Mom. "Doesn't it worry you?"

Mom kisses the top of Baby Me's head. "Why? Little Elle is perfect."

My heart soars. I could listen to Mom call me *perfect* forever.

"I'm not referring to your child," states Nal'Adel. "It's your fairy tale life template that concerns me. Elle will walk the same path as you have. A Cinderella's future is never bright."

I can't believe this. I might actually agree with Nal'Adel on this. After all, I spent most of my life avoiding becoming a servant to my sicko stepfamily. Nal'adel makes a good point.

"Don't try to ruin my good mood," says Mom. "It won't work. Like I always say, *worrying about tomorrow only ruins today*."

A pang of envy moves through me. This is such classic Rae. She flits through life, reminding me of a stone that skips over water. Mom has the gift of reflecting sunshine as she moves along, but never worrying about any eventual plunge into chilly reality.

Nal'Adel steps closer and inhales deeply over Baby Me's head. I know what this move means. Fae can scent power.

"Your baby has barely any magic," says Nal'Adel.

I can't help but smile. That's a pretty satisfying declaration, right there. In truth, I was born with an ass-ton of power. I'm the warden of all fae magic.

Sadly, that fact also made me a huge target for anyone who wants to drain my power. All of which is why Colonel Mallory the Magnificent got involved. In a totally not-shocking move, the Colonel decided my parents wouldn't be able to protect me from every power-hungry creep in Faerie. So the Colonel took away my wings and cast a spell to hide my magic from ethically-challenged folks like Nal'Adel.

On reflex, I rub my shoulder. My wings are long gone. Even so, I miss them sometimes.

Mom laughs. "What nonsense," she counters. "I'm part of the Magicorum and so is my baby. By definition, it means we both have some magic inside us."

"Just not a lot."

"You're such a grouch," states Mom. "If you don't think I've enough magic, then go find another Cinderella to serve." Mom flashes Nal'Adel a look that says, *buzz off.*

"Sometimes I wish I could," says Nal'Adel. "But you know my magical limitations. It's so hard on me."

"So you've said, many times." Mom follows this up with a laser-bright glare toward Nal'Adel.

At this point, I wish I had a lounge chair and some popcorn. I always loved seeing Mom get sassy. Mostly, she unleashed at vendors who tried to cheat our artists out of money. But watching Rae let loose on Nal'Adel? What I wouldn't give for a camera.

"Please don't take offense," says Nal'Adel silkily. "You see, my Moonshadow powers force me to see the future. They've also directed me to revitalize the Seelie empire. I'm a good person, really. My only concern is for the welfare of all Faerie."

What a load of crap. My buddy, Jacoby, is an elf prince. He told me about the Seelie and Unseelie Empires. All kingdoms align to one side or the other. In Jacoby's case, his particular kingdom, the Fortitude, serves the Unseelie empire. That makes Jacoby a dark fae. In other words, he's more likely to kill you. Not that the Seelie avoid all murder; they just do it less often.

Sadly, both the Seelie and Unseelie imperial families died

out in a massive war. Ever since then, Faerie has been a major *free for all.* It's that lawlessness which got most of Jacoby's older brothers murdered. Poor guy.

In my opinion, bringing back the Seelie would be a good thing. They're less bloodthirsty and more likely to establish order. But Nal'Adel doesn't care about anything like that. My guess is that she's "helping the Seelie" in order to become Empress herself.

Hey, it's what I'd do if I were evil as hell.

Before me, Nal'Adel keeps pleading her case to Mom. "To help all of Faerie, I must find the keeper of the opposite power to my Unseelie moonshadow magic. It's called moonbeam energy and the woman who wields it is named Kir'Adel. Once I find her, I can take in her magic and restore the Seelie Empire."

"Good for you." That's what Mom says. Her tone adds that she thinks Nal'Adel is full of crap.

Not that I blame Mom for being wary. After all, who cares what happens in Faerie anyway?

When Nal'Adel next speaks, she lowers he voice to a level that I can only call *bone chilling.* "According to my magic, you are the one who will lead me to Kir'Adel and her moonbeam magic. It's why I shall never quit you, my sweet Rae."

I do a double take. My mother will help find this Kir'Adel... all so Nal'Adel can take over as Seelie Empress? Why didn't this never came up in family conversations?

I shake my head. *Correction; I know exactly how this little tidbit of information got skipped.* If Mom thought something was nonsense, then she just brushed it aside.

"Not this again." Mom makes a tut-tut noise. "I've told you a thousand times, I do not know anyone named Kir'Adel. I'm sorry that she holds your moon-whatever, but there's nothing I can do."

"My visions say that if Kir'Adel isn't your daughter, then she's someone close to you. Think hard, Rae. This girl is the key to everything."

My skin prickles over in shock. It's one thing to discover that an evil elf queen is both your family's fairy godmother and a megalomaniac who's trying to take over the Seelie Empire. It's another matter to find out that one of your family members might be critical to her schemes.

"Elle is not this Kir person." Mom cuddles Baby Me closer. "You said yourself that my daughter doesn't have enough magic."

"That's not what I meant." Nal'Adel folds her arms over her chest. "Tell me about your friend, Marchesa. She has two girls, does she not?"

My stomach tumbles. I never thought of Ivy and Agatha as anything but pains in my neck (mostly because they were forever blowing off their chores at Cynder Mercantile.) Has something bigger been going on all this time?

"Yes, Marchesa has two children. Her youngest, Agatha, is the same age as Elle."

"I've cast divining spells on both of Marchesa's daughters, but to no avail. They have almost no magic… or someone is hiding their abilities from me."

Mom rolls her eyes. "Marchesa is not concealing anything from you."

"How can you be so certain?" Nal'Adel's mouth thins to an angry line. "Perhaps one of Marchesa's offspring is really a changeling."

Changeling. The word spins through my mind. That's when a human child is replaced by an elf baby.

Memories spin through my head. When I was at my lowest point, someone magically helped me fight Marchesa and reach the Glass Slipper Ball. Based on what Nal'Adel is saying, one of Marchesa's daughters may have had the power to make that happen. Still, it couldn't have been Ivy. That girl put the *ding* in *ding*bat.

Was it Agatha?

After all, Ivy was always the nasty one. Agatha's thing was to silently lurk in corners while wearing floppy hats and over-large sunglasses.

Those hats...

Could Agatha have been hiding her elf ears, just as she concealed the rest of herself under layers of clothing? It's totally possible.

Mom speaks again, snapping my out of my thoughts.

"Changelings?" asks Mom. "I don't think so. I was there for both of Marchesa's births. She lives by iron train tracks. The fae don't come around there, let alone swap out babies."

Nal'Adel lifts her chin. "Marchesa doesn't stay by trains all day long, you know."

Mom sighs once more. "It's always nice to see you. But if you don't have anything else to discuss, then I must return to inspecting this building. My husband and I might purchase it and create a store."

"Beware," declares Nal'Adel. "Marchesa is not a good friend for you, especially now that you're building up this enterprise. Mark my words, she'll come sniffing about for a job."

"Oh, that." Mom shrugs. "She already did. Marchesa's

husband ran off. We'll help her out. She must make a living somehow."

"That's a terrible idea!" counters Nal'Adel. "It will result in pain for you and those you love." Although as she says that as a warning, I can't help but notice how Nal'Adel looks extraordinarily pleased at the prospect of Mom suffering.

A knowing glint shines in Rae's eyes. "I already told you. I live in today."

With those words, my envy melts into something darker. Rae is just being her sunny self, and I certainly grew up happily coddled within her warmth. But unlike Mom, I also know that you can joyfully skip your ass into oncoming traffic. Sauntering blissfully into trouble doesn't make you any less dead.

I vowed I wouldn't become like that. All my life, I've fought against my fairy tale life template.

A face appears in my mind. Skye. She's the genie who's convinced that I'm fated to become one as well. I never had a true and useful fairy godmother myself. Yet seeing Mom today raises a ton of questions.

Do true Cinderellas always share Mom's motto and never worry about tomorrow?

Am I really meant to be a genie?

Or could I be permanently broken? After all, I lost my wings, which are central to the fae. Maybe other stuff got derailed at the same time.

After Mom gets saucy with Nal'Adel, the evil elf takes off

for wherever she hangs out when she's not imprisoning other people's boyfriends. I'm left to follow Mom and Baby Me around as they check out the empty warehouse. I spend a lot of time obsessing about Alec. It all circles back to one fact.

This spell sucks.

I'm supposed to be saving my boyfriend, not trotting around through time. Fascinating as it is to take a trip through my past, Alec could be drinking mud from a puddle right now. Or worse.

I try not to imagine what that *worse* could be. Too bad I have an awesome imagination.

Eventually, a different crop of questions appear in my head. This time, they're about Agatha.

Who is she, really?

Is Agatha safe from Nal'Adel?

And where is my stepsister right now?

CYNDER MERCANTILE

6

AGATHA

I stand before Cynder Mercantile, the place where I grew up. It used to be a brightly-painted storefront that showed off the coolest knick-knacks in the city. Now it's nothing but boarded-up windows and faded graffiti.

What a mess.

A few weeks ago, I visited Faerie and discovered my heritage as an elf. Ever since then, I've been living in Cynder Mercantile and looking for paperwork. With my mother and sister gone, who actually owns this place? Me, Elle, someone else? I'm on a mission to discover the truth.

Today, I finally found the records room. I could check through everything right away, but the place is dark and filled with cockroaches.

At least, that's my story and I'm sticking to it.

So instead of going through old papers, I'm off on a walk to get some coffee. Stepping away from the ruined storefront, I turn down the deserted street.

That's when I feel it. Someone is watching me.

Chances are, it's Jacoby. He's an elf prince and my personal nemesis. Also, his regular attempts at conversation are the highlight of my day.

I know. Complicated.

One thing is for certain. I do not care how I look for someone like Jacoby. It's simply a coincidence that I check my reflection in a nearby store window.

Normally, I'm a stooped figure in a boxy dress with dark hair and a floppy hat. I'm still working the dress and hat thing, only my hair is seriously different. These days, red tresses pop out from under the brim. After I found out my true heritage as an elf, my appearance changed slightly.

Anyway, I definitely look presentable.

"Jacoby, is that you?" I try hard to make my voice sound irritated, but I don't do a great job. It's lonely sitting in Cynder Mercantile. I'm constantly surrounded by dust bunnies and bad memories. If Jacoby didn't invite himself along to my nightly coffee runs, I wouldn't have any human interaction. Sure, all I do is tell him to leave me alone, but it's still the highlight of my day.

Did I mention our non-relationship is complicated? *It is.*

Sure enough, Jacoby steps out from a nearby alley. He's unnaturally handsome with his broad shoulders, aristocratic cheekbones and cute swoop of black hair. Guess that goes along with being elf royalty. You always look camera-ready.

The prince leans against the building's facade and kicks his right ankle across his left. "You really need to stop following me. It's rather embarrassing."

"*I'm* following *you?*" I try to look offended. Again, I'm not sure I do such a great job.

"It's all right." Jacoby gives me the dazzling kind of smile only the elves can pull off. "I forgive you. You can even buy me a coffee."

"I'm not talking to you or buying coffee with you." I tap my chest. "This is me, living my own life. I get that you're an elf prince and all your older brothers have been murdered—"

"Not all," says Jacoby smoothly. "Only most. And that's how things go in elf court. You'll find out for yourself soon enough. As the last Moonbeam elf, you're de facto royalty. Hail to the Queen."

"See?" I throw my hands up. "That's what I'm talking about. I want nothing to do with royal life. I'll stay right here in my old home and build up my future as a regular human." I lift my chin. "This is who I am now."

Rattling noises echo up the street. I spin about, looking for the source of the sound.

It's coming from home.

I race back to find that all hell is breaking loose at Cynder Mercantile. The entire front wall of the store shimmies with power. Light shines out from behind the planks which keep the door in place. Thin beams cut through the breaks in the wood to cast odd shadows around me.

Suddenly, the door collapses on itself, revealing a space that's filled with brightness. I'm too stunned to anything but stare into the light. The world seems to flip. Gravity no longer drags me toward the sidewalk. Instead, I'm pulled into the open door and its flickering beams.

It all happens so fast, I don't even have a chance to scream.

7

JACOBY

One second, Agatha is here.

The next, she's gone.

That's a magical transport spell, pure and simple. But who cast it? Raising my arms, I pull on the power inside me. My elf energy solidifies into an orb of light that hovers between my outstretched palms.

"Show me Agatha," I whisper.

Inside the sphere, I see Agatha standing inside a colorful temple. Columns line the walls. A checkerboard-style pattern covers the floor. A woman stands before a golden bowl.

I know this place. Agatha has been pulled into Faerie. And she's visiting none other than Eone, one of the Essentials who created the fae. Agatha stands at the center of the temple floor, her face pale with surprise. Meanwhile, Eone drags her fingertips across the surface of a water bowl.

The situation doesn't appear dangerous. Yet.

The Essentials are four powerful ladies that created Faerie out of nothing. Each has her own specialty in terms of magic. For Eone, it's time. She picks a certain outcome that she wants to happen, then Eone tries to control the cascade of events that lead to it.

For now, Eone seems calm. My bet is that she won't hurt Agatha inside the temple. Unfortunately, Eone is known for handing out rather dangerous quests. So trouble is coming to Agatha, one way or another.

A burst of protective energy runs through me. Agatha just found out she's the last of the moonbeam elves. That's not an easy adjustment. Ever since she returned to New York, Agatha has been hiding inside Cynder Mercantile. And now Eone wants to task her out with a quest? Unacceptable.

I force in a series of slow breaths. *Stay calm, Jacoby.* Agatha is a capable woman. I must wait for her to return and find out what Eone wants. Because when it comes to Essentials, it's always something big.

EONE

8

AGATHA

One second, I'm tumbling through bright and empty space. The next thing I know, I stand inside a temple. Blue light shines out from golden sconces. Hieroglyphs cover the walls in odd patterns. Other runes mark the black and white squares on the floor.

Before me, there stands a woman in a blue toga. Her hair is piled atop her head and decorated with red flowers. A golden bowl of water sits before her. Her features are so beautiful and even, she simply must be an elf.

"Where am I?" I ask.

"This is the Temple of Ages," she replies. "It's located in the Land of Faerie. And I am an Essential. Do you know what that is?"

"I've heard the stories. Essentials are supposed to have created everything in Faerie." I shift my weight from foot to foot. "But I didn't think Essentials were real."

"We are more than real, we're reality itself." The lady slowly brushes her fingers across the surface of the water. "It all started us four, the Essentials of Magic. I am Eone, the

Essential of Time. Along with my sisters, we created the great Seelie and Unseelie Empires. Then came the wars. Both imperial families were wiped out. Their vassal courts went astray."

The temple walls seem to press in more closely. "Why are you telling me all this?"

"You know that Jacoby is a Prince of the Fortitude?

"Sure."

"His kingdom wields the power of large creatures. It's also a vassal to the Unseelie Empire. Jacoby's opposite power is the Miniscule, who are aligned with the Seelie. But now? Both the Fortitude and the Minuscule are adrift. Murderous. Evil. We must bring back the Seelie and Unseelie imperial families and true ruling empires. That way, Faerie will have structure and peace."

One word of that speech pops out to me in big red letters. "We?"

Someone clears their throat nearby. I can't find it inside me to look or care. There are all sorts of enchanted lamps and pools around here. Eone must have servants who take care of these things.

In other words, whatever's happening behind my back is not as important as the Essential mess before me.

For her part, Eone hangs her head. "Not again. Damned genies."

A jolt of surprise moves through me. Inch by inch, I turn around. A woman waits behind me. From the waist up, she looks like a Marshal from the Old West, what with her black duster, silver star and cowboy hat. But where legs should be, there's only a swirl of mist.

She's definitely a genie.

Unlike the Essentials, I do know that genies are real. There are just so few of them, I never expected to meet one.

The woman tips her hat, revealing how her blonde hair is tied back in a pony tail. Her blue eyes pin me with hidden intentions.

"Howdy, Little Miss! My name is Skye."

My mouth seems to move on its won. "Okay."

Skye winks. "You don't know me, but I'm friends with your stepsister, Elle."

So this situation was already strange. But now Elle's *genie friend* is here? This revelation makes me want to return to Cynder Mercantile and check all that paperwork.

"I have an idea," says Eone. "Why don't you go *watch over Elle* right now?"

"Don't be dramatic." Skye rolls her eyes. "Elle doesn't need me to watch over her twenty-four/seven. She's fine. Besides, Elle is locked up inside her own magic right now. It's all good, right?" Skye looks to me.

"Uh, I'm not happy with how Eone says the words, *watch over Elle*. I always picture my stepsister as running around and kicking ass. But the way Eone spoke? I'm thinking Elle may be in serious trouble. Is she okay?"

"To answer that, I must flip upside down." Skye does so, and her misty bottom-half starts to spread across the ceiling in a cloud. "Elle just finished taking a magical trip down memory lane. She's got another journey coming up. Long story *longer,* your stepsister must spend time in the past before I chat up her future as a genie. Plus she must rescue her boyfriend who's trapped inside a necklace. The end."

Turns out, it isn't easy having a discussion with someone when they're upside down, leaking smoke, and talking in riddles. Everyone knows that genies are a little odd. Looks like those tales are absolutely true.

"What happened to Alec?" I ask. "Is he safe?"

"Let's just say *you* have a lot more to worry about than Elle or Alec." Skye's smoky bottom half glows with red light. "You're in deep trouble, honey."

Eone snaps her fingers. "That's enough, Skye. Stop being intimidating."

"If you insist." Skye flips upright and stops shining with crimson light. "I'll try to explain things again." She focuses on me. "You just got a whole mess of info about being an elf. Then Eone drags you in here." She shoots a sideways glance at Eone. "Which is a total lame-ass move."

Eone sets her fists on her hips. "I was just explaining things to Agatha when you barged in. I'm an Essential of magic. You should show me some respect."

Skye makes her eyes turn into swirly pools. "Whoop de doo. I'm a genie. I made a whole mess of sacrifices for this gig, so you know what that means?"

Eone sighs. "You can bother me whenever you want."

"Precisely." Skye sticks out her tongue at Eone. "Especially when you're running on your mouth."

With that, it's official. The mojo between these two is unbelievable. Ivy and I don't bicker too often, but when we do, it's a lot like this. I know from experience that the chatter can go on for hours unless someone steps in.

"Guys," I state. "Can you get to the bottom line here?"

Skye rubs her palms together. "Okay, Honey Bunches. Here's the deal. Eone saved some of the Seelie imperial family. Her favorites didn't die."

Eone nods. "True. They're all trapped inside crystals that have yet to be created."

Skye cups her hand beside her mouth. "I rarely give Eone any props, but *that* is a very cool spell."

"Thank you," states Eone. "My casting skills are indeed superb."

Skye rubs her hands together so fast, red smoke twists up from between her palms. I can't decide if her wacky antics are fun or annoying... Although I'm leaning toward the *irritating* side of things.

"Now," declares Skye. "Our Essential girl showed you her dish, right?"

"Excuse me!" Eone gestures across bowl. "This is the sacred Vessel of Hours."

"Right." Skye rolls her eyes. Turns out, she does this a lot. "So if *someone special* fills this dish up with water and then drops a certain rock inside it—"

"It's called the Eye of the World," corrects Skye.

"Yes, that rock." Skye rolls her eyes in different directions this time. "The *special someone* puts the rock in the dish along with a little water and—VOILA—the Seelie imperial family is back."

Long seconds pass as both Eone and Skye stare at me expectantly. It seems like I'm supposed to say something here. So that's what I do.

I shrug. "That's nice."

"Nice?" Skye's body balloons into double the size. "That's all you have to say?"

I hold my arms up with my palms facing forward. "Don't get me wrong. I hope you guys get the Seelie imperials back or whatever. It's just that I'm a New Yorker. So unless you plan to do something to Midtown Manhattan, I don't see how it effects me."

"We didn't tell you?" asks Giant Skye.

"This is why you're a nuisance," says Eone. "You should have let me explain."

Skye shrinks back to regular size. "Agatha, you are the *special someone* I talked about before. It's your job to bring back the Seelie imperial family. Right now, Nal'Adel is running around Faerie, looking for that dish and rock."

"They're called the Vessel of Hours and the Eye of the World," says Eone in a sing-song voice.

I exhale a long breath. "Cool. From what you're saying, Nal'Adel isn't looking for me right now. Which is great. I'm the last of the Moonbeam court. With the Vessel and Eye to distract her, Nal'Adel won't try to steal my power for her own."

"About that..." Skye winces. "*Normally*, Nal'Adel would only want to take your power."

I tilt my head. "What do you mean, *normally*?"

"Congratulations." Eone opens her arms wide. "You have a glowing mark on your hip."

On reflex, my hand goes to the spot where my tattoo hides. It doesn't glow all the time, but it is super unusual all the same.

"That mark means magic has chosen you," continues Eone. "Simply put, you're the only one who can use the Vessel of Time and the Eye of the World to bring back the Seelie imperial family."

"In other words," adds Skye. "Nal'Adel still wants to drain your magic, only she'll do it to become the chosen one herself and then restart the Seelie Empire."

I narrow my eyes and think this through. "So if I gave Nal'Adel my magic, then she could do this quest and bring back the imperials on her own?"

Eone and Skye share a long and quiet stare. Suddenly, I miss all the bickering. With these two, silence is not good.

"You can't be separated from your magic and live," says Skye simply.

I frown. "So there's no way I can hand over my magic." *What a downer.* "Got it."

"And Nal'Adel doesn't want to bring back the Seelie imperials," states Eone. "She wants to consume their magic, the same way she plans to take in your powers. And once she does that? Nal'Adel will become an Empress who's stronger than even me and Skye."

You know the phrase, *stick a fork in me, I'm done?* That's how I'm feeling right now. Still, I try to rally and process what's happening.

"Let me get this straight," I begin. "I'm not only an elf, I'm the last of the moonbeam elves."

"And a changeling," adds Eone.

My eyes widen with shock. "A what?"

"Marchesa's second baby died, you were swapped in," explains Skye. "Keep going, Hun."

Gah. Every time I think I'm getting my arms around this nightmare, something new comes up.

"Correction," I continue. "I'm an elf *changeling*. I also have a special mark that means I'm the only one who can bring back the Seelie imperial family. Why me? Why now?"

"Well, the Vessel of Time has been around for ages," says Eone. "There's always been a chosen one running around with the tattoo as well. But it's only recently that magic crystals started regrowing on the Seelie ruins, including the Eye of the World. Not sure why that's happening at this very moment, but there you go."

"And that's your quest in a nutshell," announces Skye. "Just put the rock in the dish, then the Seelie imperial family will return and it's all good. Oh, and don't get killed by Nal'Adel along the way."

I hug my elbows. "I'll think about it." *In other words, I am so not ready for this.*

"Look, Babe," says Skye. "Magic picked you. Yay. You're going to finish this quest, one way or another. Now you can get dragged along, or you can play nicely with others. What's it going to be?"

I decide that now is a great time to stare at the patterns in the floor. "Still thinking."

Eone rounds on Skye. "I knew this would happen if you showed up. I had everything under control. I was going to do a big show for Agatha with the Vessel and Eye. Now things will be even more unpleasant for her."

The two start bickering again, only much louder this time. All of a sudden, I feel a gentle breeze against my back. Turning around, I find Jacoby standing behind me. *Good.* His silhouette is also framed by an open portal that leads back to Manhattan. *Even better.*

"Ready to go?" asks Jacoby.

"Absolutely."

Stepping through Jacoby's door, I quickly leave Skye and Eone behind. Sadly, I doubt that walking out on their quest will be as easy.

9

JACOBY

I guide Agatha through the portal and away from the crazy magical ladies. Moments later, we stand in front of Cynder Mercantile once more.

Agatha shoots me a shy glance. "Why did you do that?"

"What?"

Her cheeks turn a cute shade of pink. "Come and get me."

"It seemed like you'd had enough. Besides, Eone and Skye were done. Once they start yelling at the same time, it's all over."

Agatha looks up. In the streetlights, her irises shine a vivid shade of green. "You knew I was with them?"

I nod. "Once you vanished from the sidewalk, I cast a spell to check on you. I couldn't hear what they said, but I knew where you were."

Agatha's forehead crinkles as she thinks this through. "So that spell is like watching a movie with the sound off."

"Pretty much." I love how Agatha is so curious about magic. She asks lots of questions. One day, she'll be a fine caster.

Agatha hugs her elbows. "I need to get some rest now."

"And I must insist that I see you safely inside Cynder. After you're settled in, I can cast a few protection spells. You won't be bothered again tonight."

Agatha sighs. "Thank you."

In truth, I could cast all the protection spells I want from the sidewalk. But my kingdom is aligned to the Unseelie Empire, which means that I'm a bit of an asshat. And this the most Agatha's allowed me to talk to her since we left Faerie.

Not that I blame her for putting distance between us. I made a horrible mistake in not trusting her before. If it takes forever, I will make it up to her. And if that doesn't work, then I'll just keep on being sneaky.

I step closer. "Do you want to talk about what happened at the temple?"

Agatha shakes her head.

"I understand. Now close your eyes and picture where you want to go." Agatha squishes her eyes shut. It's adorable. "Do you know where the portal should take us?"

Agatha nods.

I lift my arms and summon another sphere of power. The orb of colored magic expands into a stone archway that sits in the center of the sidewalk.

"The spell is ready," I announce.

Agatha opens her eyes. "Thanks."

Together, Agatha and I step through the passage and into a rather creepy place.

And considering my life, that's really saying something.

CYNDER

10

JACOBY

*F*or a while, it's all I can do to soak in my surroundings. I stand in a rickety attic filled with odd and unsettling toys. For instance, there's an entire shelf dedicated to nothing but laughing clown dolls.

What this says about Agatha's childhood is a lot.

"Where are we?" I ask.

"It's my old playroom growing up. I didn't want to picture my bedroom." She turns pink once more. "This place is, uh, much better."

"Seriously?" I gesture toward the shelf of maniacal clowns. "Excuse me for saying so, but this room is creepy as fuck."

Agatha tries to hide a smile. I'm so getting to her, it isn't even funny. "Maybe."

"Please. I live with a minotaur and a herd of monsters. I know when something is unsettling. And this place is deeply disturbing." I scan a nearby bookshelf and pick up an old copy of *Grimm's Fairy Tales*.

Agatha gasps. "Don't read that!"

"I'm the Prince of the Fortitude. My people are vassals to

the Empire of Unseelie fae. I positively worship the dark side of elf nature."

Agatha rolls her eyes. "As if there's really a light side."

"In other words, I'm aboslutely reading this." I open the cover and recite the inscription aloud.

Agatha,

The power of magicorum drags normal humans like us away from our regular lives and into cruel fairy tale templates. That's why you'll never be anything more than an evil stepsister to an even more deplorable Cinderella.

Never forget that.

-Marchesa

"Oh, my." I snap the book closed. "Your mother is such a bitch."

"She's not my mother."

"When did you discover this little fact?"

"During my visit to the temple."

"And?"

"I'm not telling you anything more."

"That's fine. I'll keep looking through your old toys." I flip around. "Oh, wow! A shelf of evil clowns. Let's play." I pull off a lanky number with overly large eyes and shoes. "Hello, Agatha." I make him wave, a motion that sets off a cascade of cobwebs. "Now watch me dance!"

Agatha chuckles. "Fine. I'll talk. Just put away the clown."

I dutifully reset the doll on the shelf. *If I never touch that thing again, I'll be a happy elf.*

"Here's what I learned," continues Agatha. "I'm one hundred percent elf. A changeling. That elf essential, Eone, and some unhinged genie, Skye, want me to bring back the Seelie imperial family... which Eone has saved inside crystals for just such an occasion. Oh, and I must do all this without letting Nal'Adel become an Empress herself or kill me."

I tap my lips with my finger and consider this turn of events. For years, there have been rumors that the Essentials saved both the Seelie and Unseelie imperial families. I assumed it was wishful thinking. If it's real, it's a chance for some fools to get killed while another evil person becomes Empress.

Ah, well. With any luck, this is someone else's problem. "What specific words did Eone use?" I ask. "Did she give you a formal quest?"

Agatha kicks at the floor. When she speaks, her voice is little more than a peep. "No.

"You're a deplorable liar."

"Fine. They did give me a quest. I must take Eone's dish—"

"That would be the Vessel of Time."

"And place in a rock."

"The proper name is the Eye of the World."

"And mix them together. If I do that, all the nice Seelie that Eone likes will come back to the imperial palace."

I lift my brows, impressed. "Based on that spell, Eone must have placed her favorite Seelie into magical crystals that wouldn't grow until a future date. Clever. Then again, she is an Essential." I focus on Agatha once more. "And did you accept this quest?"

"No way! I am not running around Faerie looking for a bowl and a rock."

"No complaints here. Restarting the Seelie Empire only complicates politics for the Unseelie vassals like mine. Although…"

"What?"

"If they assigned you this task, then there's no way to get around it."

Agatha pales. "I can't do this quest! I'm not strong enough." She gestures toward the copy of *Grimm's Fairy Tales*. "You know why Marchesa gave me that book? I hit honor roll once in middle school. That inscription is a warning for me to never succeed. Ivy's the one who should shine. And after that book, I failed on purpose and never got honor roll again. I gave up on myself." Her voice cracks. "That's how weak I am."

Sadness presses in around me. *My sweet Agatha.*

"I disagree," I state gently. "All that time, you concealed incredible power. Such control takes strength."

Agatha keeps staring at the floor. I set my knuckle under her chin. Bit by bit, I guide her gaze to meet mine. "Did it ever occur to you that if you were really weak, then they wouldn't have spent so much time trying to convince you of that fact?"

Agatha's lower lip wobbles. "I'm still not up for this."

"Are you resolved to live here, then?"

"Yes. I want a normal life in New York without Marchesa and Ivy. With them gone, this building could be mine."

My chest warms with affection and awe. *What a woman.* Who else would turn down both an essential and a genie to build up her own future?

Agatha tilts her head. "Why are you smiling?"

"Because you really are a wonder." I rub my thumb across

her chin and then lower my hand. "I'll see you tomorrow night at our non-date for coffee."

A spark of humor lights Agatha's emerald eyes. "And I won't care either way."

"Of course."

I can't help but grin. When it comes to Agatha, I'm definitely making progress.

AGATHA

*J*acoby opens another portal. This one looks like a stone arch and is set into the wall itself. He takes a half-step toward the magical exit, pauses, and turns toward me once more. "Did Skye or Eone say anything about Elle?"

A new feeling burns inside me. It feels a lot like jealousy.

Don't be a doofus, Agatha. Elle and the prince are just friends. Nothing more. The fact that Jacoby used to moon all over Elle for years means zero.

Maybe if I keep repeating that, I'll start to believe it.

I realize that I've been staring at Jacoby for too long and not saying anything. I clear my throat. "Skye said something about Elle traveling to the past." I snap my fingers. "Oh, and that Elle has to rescue her boyfriend who is trapped in a necklace."

Jacoby narrows his eyes. "Nal'Adel must have placed Alec inside a gemstone prison."

"So that means something to you? It just came across as a lot of gibberish to me."

"If I had to guess," begins Jacoby. "I'd say Elle is on a quest of her own. In her case, she must free Alec from this magical prison." He refocuses on me. All of a sudden, I can imagine how a bug feels when a magnifying glass shoots a beam of light in its face. "Did Skye or Eone seem worried about Elle?"

"Eone sounded concerned. Skye wasn't anxious at all, though. The genie did say one odd thing though—that Elle was locked in her own magic."

Jacoby exhales. "That's good news."

"Really? What does it mean?"

"Elle is new to casting. Sometimes you use too much power in a spell, and it can take you out of space and time for a while. She'll be back soon enough." His focus swings back to me again. I have the instinct to pull my floppy hat down around my chin.

"I was so worried," Jacoby says in a low voice.

"About Elle?"

"No." Jacoby steps closer. "About *you*."

Every cell in my body seems to freeze. This is Jacoby. He's the handsome prince who worships the ground Elle walks on. And for some reason, he's concerned about me. I can only manage to whisper a single word.

"Why?"

"I didn't think Skye or Eone would hurt you physically, but there's been too much happening in your life lately. Someone must watch out for you."

The room seems to collapse into a bubble until there's only me and Jacoby. Heat rises between us. And the whole scene scares the crap out of me.

"I'm fine," I say quickly. "I'll get some rest now. I found some papers. I need to read them in the morning. It's a thing."

Jacoby takes a half-step toward the portal. "Coffee tomorrow night?" he asks.

"We covered this already," I reply. "There is zero chance of me getting coffee with you." Still, I'm smiling my face off as I say this.

He winks. "It's a date, then."

Jacoby steps through the portal. Once he's away, the stone arch blinks out of existence. With the prince gone, the playroom feels especially cold and empty.

Now that my jealousy had cooled, I can't help but wonder about Elle. When Eone talked about Elle, there was some definite worry in the Essential's voice. I'm still not thrilled about that fact. I close my eyes and send a silent message to my stepsister.

Wherever you are, Elle, please be safe.

CYNDER MERCANTILE

12

ELLE

J follow Mom and Baby Me around different parts of the empty building. Along the way, Rae comments on stuff like electrical fixtures and water damage. It sounds pretty technical. Mostly I focus on how Baby Me coos and is adorable.

I'm not sure how long this goes on, but eventually some mist billows across the floor. Within seconds, the entire chamber is filled with a magical cloud.

Been here, seen this.

When I first entered Cynder, the place looked all foggy as well. If this is like last time, then the misty thing won't last for long.

Sure enough, the cloud fades to reveal that I'm still inside the warehouse of Cynder Mercantile. Mom and Baby Me are gone. Something other things have changed, too. One wall of the room now holds a garden and a door, just like the portal that first brought me here.

So far, so good.

This little trip through time was unexpected, but it wasn't

useless. There were a lot of wins here in the *stuff I need to know* column. I count them off in my head.

First, I'm now aware that Nal'Adel is scheming to become the empress of a newly-returned Seelie super-kingdom.

Second, Nal'Adel needs the magic of her opposite, Kir'Adel, in order to bring the Seelie back.

Third, the smart money is on the fact that Kir'Adel is actually Agatha. Knowing how Nal'Adel works, the process of 'taking Kir's magic' will not be fun or pleasant.

Four, the fact that Alec is trapped in Nal'Adel's prison means all these other insights could be very useful, very soon.

A thread of worry twists through my chest. Before, I was mostly concerned about freeing Alec. And although being imprisoned sucks, it can't be as bad as having a bloodthirsty elf after you who wants to drain-n-kill you ASAP.

I must find Agatha and check on her.

Best call up more magic.

Focusing inside my soul, I sense the power churning within me. Since it worked so well last time (relatively speaking) I decide to yell at my magic once more.

"Get out here!"

Torrents of pink sparkles pour off my hands and spin about the floor, whirlpool style.

"I must help Agatha!"

The mists billow and expand until they fill the entire warehouse. Then they vanish. Another portal appears halfway across the room. It's more of a black hole that sinks into the wall. A dark form hovers in the opening. My eyes widen as I take in the creature before me. It's a floating torso with glowing eyes and a rasping voice.

"Elle Cynder," it begins. "Nal'Adel is displeased with you."

"Well, she's not my favorite chick either right now."

I glance toward the far wall. My garden-style doorway is still open, but the new portal-n-creature combo have set up shop half-way to that exit. All of a sudden, my vista door is looking pretty sweet. Sadly, the worst thing you can do with a predator is haul ass across its path in order to escape.

So I stand stock-still and wait to see what the monster will do next.

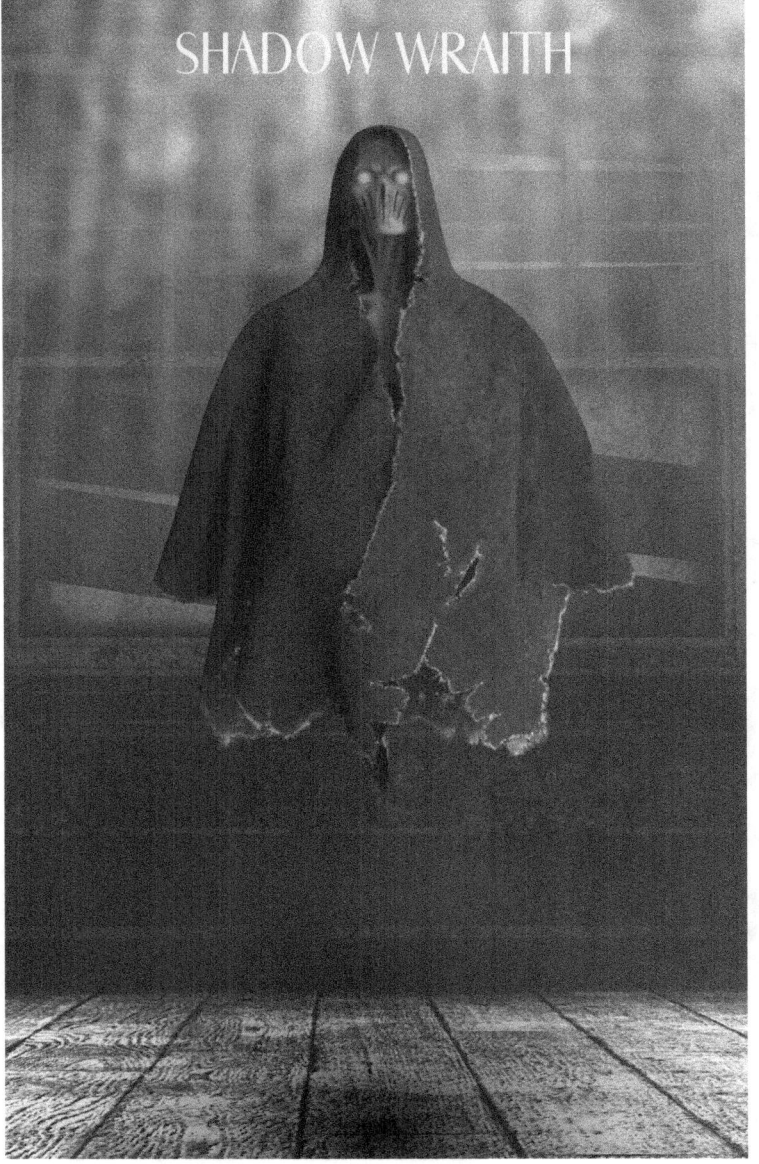

13

ELLE

*N*ow, in order to un-steal jewelry, I occasionally have to run a con. It's an unexpected and totally rare side effect of my profession.

Actually, that's a major lie.

I run heavy cons all the time. So much so, I've developed a list of rules for interacting with marks. One such guideline is this...

Get the target talking.

Unfortunately, after announcing that Nal'Adel is not pleased with yours truly, Torso Guy has stayed annoyingly silent.

Time to change that.

"So, what should I call you?" I ask. "Floaty dude? Head-n-Shoulders? That could be like Salt-n-Pepa, only a lot less cool."

"I am a Shadow Wraith. I have no name."

"Okay, Wraith. I'm Elle."

"I am aware of this fact."

At this point, it takes everything in me not to cheer. *Wraith is a chatty guy!* This will be fun.

"I come from Nal'Adel," adds the Wraith.

"Are you here to bring back my boyfriend?"

"No. I am here to deliver a message. Nal'Adel wishes you to leave Agatha alone."

I smack my lips and consider this turn of events. There's no missing the fact that the Wraith isn't attacking. And based on his lack of social skills and legs, he's really not built to be anything but a warrior. All of which leads to a question.

"Why is Nal'Adel asking me this?"

"Because you have important friends."

"Oh." My eyes widen. "You mean Colonel Mallory."

"Yes," agrees the Wraith. "We have no desire to incur his anger."

"You know, the Colonel likes my boyfriend, Alec, too. Just saying."

"Enough to rip off his wings and hide him from the world?"

"Wow. That's just rude." *And true, not that I'll admit this to my new monster friend.* The Colonel isn't necessarily a guy hater, it's more that he has a protective instincts when it comes to the ladies.

Okay, the Colonel is totally a guy hater.

When it comes to Mallory the Magnificent, Knox and Alec are more tolerated than anything else, and that's only because of their relationships with me and Bry.

"Give up," states the Wraith. "Return home. No harm will come to you."

"About that," I state. "I *will* save both Agatha and Alec, then

I'll kick Nal'Adel's butt while pulling out her obnoxious hair extensions. What do you say about that?"

A long pause follows. The wraith's eyes keep glowing red.

"What?" I ask. "Too much?"

I guess the answer to that question is *yes,* because the Wraith flies right at me. Even worse, it turns out that the thing has long bony arms with claw-like fingers. And it's aiming those nails right for my face.

Damn. That thing can book.

I summon fresh magic from within me and raise my own arms.

"Get it!" I yell.

Cords of pink power shoot out from my palms, sticking the wraith to the wall like a bug on so many pins.

Who knew I could do that? *Not me.*

Still, it's pretty sweet.

The Wraith wriggles under the magical bolts that hold it in place. The pink cords are already starting to fray and crack.

Damn.

This can't go on for long. How many times can I shout *get it* before the Wraith figures out how to dodge my spell? And it's not like I have a ton of other things that I can cast. Right now, my full inventory of spells consists of two options: opening a portal and what I've now decided to call the Bug Pinner Special.

Oh, wait. Portal.

I still have the first one opened from before. Too bad it's on the other side of the room.

Better go fast.

Pumping my arms, I race across the very large warehouse. All the while, the Wraith twists under my magical pins.

Its right side gets loose.

I'm halfway across the room.

The wraith's left half gets loose as well.

I'm three-quarters of the way to the portal.

The wraith becomes fully free and flies straight at me with such speed, the thing is little more than a black blur. Its claw-like fingers almost grasp my hair as I leap through my portal and into a scene I'd never expected.

The Old West.

Yes, *that* Old West.

Just when I thought I'd seen all the strange things.

OLD WEST TOWN

14

ELLE

I stand at the end of a dusty street. Wooden structures loom over the dirt road. Words like *Saloon, Bank* and *Mercantile* are painted on each facade. The scent of horse manure and hay fills the air. A low murmur of voices echo inside the buildings.

Rage and frustration battle it out inside my nervous system. I need to find Alec and Agatha, not re-enact scenes from *Old Yeller*.

I pace a line along the center of the street. Little by little, my anger melts into curiosity. After all, my trip to Cynder Mercantile ended up giving me useful information. Maybe I need to trust my magic a little bit. Perhaps I need to learn a few things before I'm ready for the big rescue attempt.

Best if I stay alert and watch for opportunities. Besides, that's got to be a better plan than pacing around in circles while picturing punching Nal'Adel in the throat.

Someone steps out from the shadows onto the street itself. Shielding my eyes from the sun, I check out the newcomer.

It's a woman in an outrageously pale outfit. And even though she's dressed strangely, I'd know her anywhere.

It's Skye, only this version doesn't have mist for legs.

She's not a genie.

Yet.

SKYE

15

ELLE

I decide to call this version of my genie Dressy Skye. When strange things happen in your life, it's important to give them names.

For a minute, I just watch Dressy Skye be her own fussy self. She pats down her hair. Adjusts her hat just so. She even lifts up the edge of her skirts to avoid random splotches of water on the street. Plus, when this puddle-avoidance takes place, I discover that Dressy Skye is wearing white shoes as well. What's up with that? Did she plan to visit the Old West or a semiconductor clean room?

Dressy Skye walks up and down the street a few times. She waves at windows and tries to get someone's attention. It doesn't work. Clearly, she doesn't see me. By this point, I'm getting used to this.

Eventually, a crinkly old guy with a massive black stetson steps out of the place marked *stables.*

On a side note, I'm very impressed with the labeling ability of this town. They may not have paved streets, but whoever runs this place wields a mean stencil.

Dressy Skye marches over to the old gentleman. In the process, she walks right through me. Turns out, it's a weird sensation to have someone step through your body. And by that, I mean it tickles.

She pauses before the older guy. "Excuse me, Sir."

"Yes, Miss?" He tips his hat.

"I'm looking for Governor Morningstar. Do you know where I might find him?"

"Try the saloon."

Dressy Skye pales. "Saloon?"

"That's right. Excuse me, Miss." After tipping his hat again, the man saunters off.

This is what you call on *old fashioned turning point*. Dressy Skye doesn't look like she's ready to walk down a dusty street, let alone hang out in a saloon. Leaning back on my heel, I give her a good once-over. The Marshall Skye I know is a badass in black. She'd have no problem walking into a saloon and possibly drinking the place dry.

But this version? It's a tough call.

Eventually, Dressy Skye takes a deep breath and heads into the saloon. I follow along behind her. The building itself is a long and low space with wood floors, round tables and a player piano. There's a long bar built into the wall. No one's behind it, which isn't too much of a shocker. It's early morning and no customers have shown up yet.

Dressy Skye steps into the center of the room. "Hello." She clears her throat. "I'm Skye Morningstar. I'm here to see the Governor."

A second ago, I would have sworn this place was empty except for Dressy Skye. Now a new figure steps out from the shadows. She wears fringed leather pants and a jacket to match. Her long black hair is entwined with colorful feathers.

"I'm Governor Morningstar."

"Oh." Dressy Skye blushes. "I was expecting, um…"

"A man?" Governor shrugs. "I could take that form, if you like. It's all part of our life template."

Dressy Skye shakes her head. "I'm very confused. I was told to come here and find my kin, Governor Morningstar. You see, I'm supposed to be a Cinderella fairy tale life template, but it isn't working out."

"We are kin." Governor pulls out a bear claw necklace from under her jacket. A silver stopper sits atop the massive claw. My eyes widen. That isn't just a claw—it's a container. Governor pulls the silver top off from the clawed bottom.

Everything changes.

Governor transforms into a smoky version of herself. She spirals down into the claw container. There's no question about it. Governor is a genie and the claw is her bottle. Once Governor vanishes inside the claw, the stopper replaces itself. The necklace sits on the floor.

Dressy Skye takes a few steps closer to the claw container. "Governor?" she asks. "Are you alright?"

The stopper pops out of the claw and the process reverses. Smoke pours out from the top of the necklace and grows larger by the second. When the cloud solidifies, Governor is once again standing in the saloon.

Emotions battle it out inside me. One half of my consciousness is terrified by what I just saw. But the other side? I want me a bottle or claw of my very own. Now.

Governor nods toward Dressy Skye. "Whatever magic

drives our lives, yours and mine are the same. I see it on you, clear as the moon."

For her part, Dressy Skye sets her hand on her throat. "But I already met my prince. I'm here to get my magic fixed. That way, we can get married."

Governor waves her hands across a nearby table. A series of bottles appear. "We both know that won't happen. It's time to make your choice."

My heart sinks. I've seen images like those before. Magical bottles. They're perfect for a genie.

Is this why my magic drew me to this place? Is my fate finally revealing itself, just as it did to Skye?

ALADDIN'S CHOICE

ELLE

The moment takes on a surreal gleam. I'm not sure how I know this, but I'm certain I'm about to see the ritual that transforms a regular person into a genie.

I can't tell if I'm more terrified or overjoyed. And that's confusing as hell.

Governor folds her arms over her chest. "Which one of these will be your home in times of trouble?"

Dressy Sky takes a half-step backward. "I don't know what you mean."

Governor pulls out her bear claw necklace once more. "This is my home when I need to recharge my energy. The magic wants you to choose one of these for yourself."

"I refuse."

"Then the magic will choose for you."

Dressy Skye pats her pockets, pulling out a small silver container. "I didn't put this here."

"I told you the magic would choose." Governor steps closer. "You were given a good home. A metal bottle is practical. Not as fine as a claw, but it will do. Now all you do is choose your genie name and it's over."

"Genie name." Dressy Skye clutches the container to her chest. "Why do they call you Governor?"

"They don't call me anything. My birth name is dead to me. I chose the name Governor. And many of our kind are called Morningstar."

"But what about my prince?" Dressy Skye sets the back of her hand against her forehead. "I'm supposed to get my magic fixed so we can get married."

"You need to move on from that illusion," states Governor. "Magic always derails romance for our kind. You're here because someone saw that truth in you."

Those words slam into me with force. I stumble backward. *This can't be happening.* I'm here to try and save Alec, not give up on any chance that we can be together.

With wobbly steps, I rush out the door. And right into another version of Skye.

SKYE

ELLE

*W*hile speeding out of the saloon, I almost run directly into Skye. This time, she wears her black duster, dark hat, and silver star. I take a half-step backward.

"Can you see me?" I ask.

Skye's legs instantly transform into a swirl of smoke. "You know it, Sister."

I hitch my thumb over my shoulder. "Was that really you back in the saloon?"

"Oh, yeah. I thought I was Cinderella, same as you do. But I'm a genie."

"Did you bring me here?"

She shoots me a sly smile. "You'd like that, wouldn't you? It would be easier if *I* were dragging you into my past. That would mean *your own* magic wasn't at work."

I set my fist on my hip. "So is that a *yes* or a *no?*"

"It's a big ass *no*, sweet cakes. My powers have absolutely nothing to do with bringing you here. Although I hope you learned a thing or two." Skye reaches into her pocket and pulls out the same silver vial I saw Dressy Skye handle inside the saloon. "When it's your time, it's your time. Magic will give you a new home." She resets the vial into her pocket. "Any questions?"

I rub my neck and try to keep my mouth shut. After all, I don't really want to be a genie. But a question tumbles past my lips anyway. *Stupid mouth.*

"If someone finds your bottle, do you have to help them?"

"Nah. We choose who we want to help, end of story. You're a lucky lady, Elle. Few are selected to become a genie."

I decide to leave the *you're a lucky lady* comment alone. I certainly have felt less-than-fortunate lately. Although right now—when Skye is acting totally sane—talking with her does feel like a gift. "What about the three wishes?"

"Oh, that's just to get people off our backs. If you don't set limits, humans will never stop bugging you. So we give them a replica bottle until it's time to set them on their merry way. Anything else?"

"How many genies are there?"

Skye makes a great show of counting on her fingers. Twice. "In total? Four."

"Oh." Suddenly, the hard-core recruitment push from Skye makes a lot more sense.

"Tell me," continues Skye. "Are you ready to make the change? I can help it happen right now."

I shake my head. Sometimes, Skye comes up with stuff and there really isn't anything to say.

"Use your noggin, Elle. If you became a genie, then you could make a wish and save Alec. Problem solved."

My mind reels through this revelation. Is it really that simple? Could I just become a genie and end all this trouble?

"Say it with me," orders Skye. "Thank you, wondrous genie. All my problems are solved."

"If fixing all this is so easy, why don't you make a wish *for* me?"

She taps her chin as if seriously considering my request. "Nope. Doesn't work that way."

I think through the idea of becoming a genie. If I become one and free Alec, then I'm forever separated from my old life and future.

A sneaky light shines in Skye's eyes. "Ask me for a wish."

I haven't run cons all my life not to know when one's being pulled on me. "What's the catch?"

"You'll become a genie, of course."

"No."

Skye exhales a dramatic sigh. "Then I can't protect you, I'm afraid."

I frown. "What are you talking about?"

"You need to stay safe from Nal'Adel. You pinned her Shadow Wraith to a wall like a bug. Plus, you're still trying to help Alec and Agatha. Nal'Adel specifically told you to stop that. And if you don't let me switch you into genie-hood right now, then I can't protect you from her wrath." She twiddles her fingers. "Buh-bye."

Skye's body melts into a cloud of smoke before vanishing entirely.

For a long minute, I stand alone in the dusty street. Dark clouds roll over the skies. A heavy coating of mist rises up from the ground. Adrenaline courses through me.

Something is on its way.

Another monster steps out of the darkness. And this one is far worse than the Shadow Wraith.

LADY CLOAKE

ELLE

*N*ot too long ago, Nal'Adel sent a floating torso with pointy fingers in order to scare and-or kill me. This time, my enemy is a warrior chick with a funky collar, lots of hair, and a flap of skin over her lips.

Which raises an issue.

In situations like this one, I like to get the big-bad chatting. But since chick has no mouth? That won't be so easy.

Still, this babe can probably cover a lot of territory by using hand gestures and whatnot. Plus, she isn't attacking yet, which means she might be open to stuff... you know, other than killing me.

I can work with that.

"Hey there," I begin. "I'm Elle."

The woman lifts her hand. Like the Shadow Wraith, she has claw-like fingers. There's a big difference, though. Funky Collar Chick uses her sharp fingers to rip off whatever's covering her jawline.

Eew. Just eew.

Even worse, the motion exposes a super-wide mouth that's lined with knife-like teeth.

More than I needed to know.

"I am Lady Cloake," she says. "Nal'Adel sent me."

"Let me guess. Nal'Adel wants me to stop helping Alec and Agatha."

"Correct. Open a portal and go home. Now."

"I'll think about that." I tap my foot. "Done. The answer is *no.* Not a chance."

Lady Cloake pulls a pair of daggers from holsters on her thighs. "How unfortunate."

Yeah, I think. *For you.*

Pulling on my inner power, I summon fresh cords of power. Sparkling ropes whip out of my palms and rush toward Lady Cloake. Before, I had my magic pin my enemy to the wall. This time, I'd plan to rope her, cowgirl style. Because it's important to mix things up when you're fighting magical evildoers.

My lines of energy whip through the darkness. Just when they're about to wrap around Lady Cloake's torso, the warrior leaps high, does a somersault in mid-air, and then lands way out of the range of my magic.

Damn.

Lady Cloake tosses her daggers at me. The good news is that she has crap for aim. The blades land in the ground on either side of my feet.

Perfect.

Her storm trooper-style accuracy gives me a chance to try my magical cords again. Raising my arms, I summon more power. This time, I figure I'll launch my ropes high into the air. Maybe if they land *behind* Lady Cloake, then I can tie her up more easily.

That's not what happens.

On either side of me, the daggers glow with white power. A great orb of energy appears between them, reminding me of a giant soap bubble that sits upon a smooth tabletop. Only in this situation, the soap bubble is a prison of white magic and I'm stuck underneath it.

I slam my shoulder against the orb of power around me. The barrier doesn't even shimmy, let alone break.

Lady Cloake stands just outside the magical barrier. "You're fortunate that Nal'Adel wants you alive."

I keep trying to slam and kick my way out. "I know, she's scared of Colonel Mallory."

"Correct." Lady Cloake shoots me an over-wide grin. "Nal'Adel also wishes to control Agatha. You may come in handy for that as well." She shakes her head. "Which is too bad. Killing you would have been interesting."

A hungry gleam shines in Lady Cloake's eyes. I freeze in place. I'm well aware of that look. It's the same one I get when I'm about to make my big move. In my case, that means I'm about to grab some jewelry.

So what does Lady Cloake have planned?

The answer appears when the ground beneath me falls away. As I tumble down into darkness, Lady Cloake calls after me.

"Enjoy the gemstone prison!"

CYNDER STORAGE

19

AGATHA

he next day I spend in the storage room, going through papers. What I discover is pretty dismal. Marchesa *does* own this property, but she also has four mortgages, none of which have been paid in months. It's only a matter of time before bankers repossess everything.

I could pay things off with magic, but that's unfair to hardworking humans. It's also easily tracked. Humans have a special council that punishes rule breakers.

It's becoming more and more clear that this house is depressing and I really shouldn't be here. But where else would I go?

In the end, I decide to take a break and grab a cup of coffee. Since it's close to 2 a.m., you'd think it would be impossible to fill up on java. Good thing this is Manhattan. I happen to know the perfect spot to get caffeinated at this hour.

Hyacinth Coffee.

I step outside Cynder Mercantile and linger. There's no

sign of Jacoby. Which is fine. Who needs a princely stalker anyway?

With that lie firmly implanted in my mind, I head off to the coffee shop alone.

HYACINTH COFFEE

20

AGATHA

*H*yacinth Coffee is in a very funky part of town. After a short walk, I find the place is packed with partiers. The smell of cigarette smoke and stale booze carries on the air. At this time of night, most customers are stopping by for the equivalent of a *red hot red bull* before hitting their next bar.

The line curls around the store. I'm about to join the queue when someone grips my free hand and yanks me into a hug. "Oh, Agatha! Agatha!"

It takes me a second to realize who has grabbed me.

Marchesa. She looks as pinched and nasty as I remember. Heavy whirls of brown hair are perched atop her head. Beside her, Ivy is all bright eyes, pale hair, and an empty smile.

This is unpleasant on three levels. First, it's Marchesa. Second, she has Ivy with her. And third, she yanked me with such force, I missed my chance to get into line.

"Come along!" cries Marchesa. "Ivy and I have grabbed a table for us, right by the window."

In the movie of my life, this is where I'd go all ninja on

Marchesa's ass. Maybe I'd do one of those moves where I kick out her legs or something.

But that's not how I roll. Instead, I pull my floppy hat down around my ears and allow myself to get dragged over to a far corner of the small shop. I end up sitting with my back to the wall and the shop's main window to my right.

Ivy slips onto the chair across from mine. Marchesa takes the seat to my left. It's Ivy who speaks first. "What happened to your hair?"

"Oh." I twist a few locks around my fingers. Before, my hair had been brown. I'd forgotten how it has changed color after I'd looked into the Moonbeam Mirror. "It's red."

"Well, that shade is terrible on you," adds Ivy. "Where's your veil?"

"My hat is fine."

"You need to cover up all of that nightmarish red hair." Marchesa smirks. "I think I have some old napkins that might help."

I pinch the bridge of my nose. "I so don't need this right now."

A new voice sounds. "Leave her alone."

My breath catches. It's Jacoby.

I shoot him a sly look. "I thought you'd missed our not-a-date."

"I got distracted because I suspected someone else was following you. Turns out, I was right."

In all the drama of seeing my fake family, I didn't realize that the prince had stepped into the coffee shop. Now Jacoby stands right beside me, tall and looming.

I won't lie. That's a great place for him to be.

21

JACOBY

*J*grip the back of Agatha's chair with such force, the wood creaks. My blood heats just thinking about the nasty things this pair just said to Agatha. Sure, some may think it's only helpful comments about her floppy hat and newly-red hair, but I know the truth.

I've buried seven of my brothers. I know what hurt means. I won't tolerate anyone injuring those I care about, however they apply the pain.

Marchesa notices me. "Oh, Jacoby! I didn't see you there."

Ignoring her, I focus on Agatha. "You don't have to do this."

Agatha tilts her head, considering. After a few moments, she speaks. "It's okay. We can chat for a few minutes."

"One hundred and twenty seconds," I declare. "Just give me the word."

Long seconds tick by. Ivy is the one to break the silence next. "Mummy and I need to speak to our dear Aggie. Can you give us some privacy, Jacoby?"

"There's no way I'm leaving without Agatha's permission."

I glare between Ivy and Marchesa. "What do you two want from her?" I rest my hand on Agatha's shoulder, just so there's no question who *her* is in this situation.

"Well," says Ivy. "We're here to find bring Agatha to Faerie."

Leaning forward, Marchesa speaks in a low and conspiratorial tone. "We got a message from our mutual friend, Nal'Adel. She's assigned us a personal assistant, you know."

"She provides us information, directions and everything," gushes Ivy.

"You might remember her," says Marchesa slowly. "Her name is Lady Cloake. So will you come with us back to Faerie?"

"No," states Agatha.

"Don't be silly," says Ivy. "It's best for you to do what Nal'Adel says. You know what happened to Alec."

Agatha lifts her chin. "I'm aware. You're not the only one with allies, you know."

I brush my thumb in slow arcs on Agatha's shoulder. It's a small movement, but I hope she gets the message. *Good work, Agatha.* It's a smart play to hint at the chat with Eone and Skye. Both of them are more powerful than Nal'Adel... At least for the moment.

Ivy shakes her head dramatically. "I guess we better leave them now."

Marchesa rises slowly. "Because if you won't follow us into the Faerie Lands, perhaps the Shadow Morph can drag you back to where you belong."

It's an effort to keep my features carefully even. There's no way I can allow Marchesa, Ivy or Agatha to know how much this news disturbs me.

Because Shadow Morphs are some of the worst assassins

in Nal'Adel's employ. They turn darkness into liquid evil and are nearly impossible to kill.

I risk a glance toward the far corner of the coffee shop. Sure enough, a Shadow morph now oozes from the ceiling. She's in her stealth mode, so none of the humans can tell what about to happen.

But I know the next steps well enough.

A battle is only seconds away.

SHADOW MORPH

22

AGATHA

I follow Jacoby's line of vision. Indeed a sludgy creature drips down from the ceiling of the coffee shop. I've heard about these things, but never wanted to encounter them in real life.

A Shadow Morph.

"Agatha Cynder," says the monster. "Step inside me. I will bring you to Faerie."

This is the classic move of a Shadow Morph. They surround you in their nasty goo. From that point, they puppet you around like a marionette covered in dripping black paint.

I'll pass.

Beside me, Jacoby raises his hands to chest level and conjures a sphere of magic. Tossing the orb to the floor, it sends ripples of blue energy out across the cafe.

The humans react as a chill of fear speeds through the shop. All the patrons yelp with terror as they run for the street. Even Ivy and Marchesa take off. The cafe lies empty.

I nod, impressed. That's a pretty good spell, right there. If

Jacoby and I live through this, I'll have to ask him to teach it to me one day.

While Jacoby was doing his spell-thing, I hadn't noticed the Shadow Morph send a tendril of goo my way. Although most of her remains in the corner, there's now a line of sludge from that point to me. The gooey line rises up beside me, where it turns into a drippy hand. It's that slimy hand that now grips my own. A voice sounds in my head.

How interesting.

I'm about to shake this goopy chick off my wrist when the Shadow Morph says something even more shocking.

Are you and Jacoby bonded?

Now bonding happens when two elves share their real names. Their souls become linked. It's like human marriage on elfy steroids. And it's nothing I'd ever consider with Jacoby. So I freak out.

"WHAT?" I say, and my voice is maybe an octave or two higher than normal. "We're not bonded." I yank my arm free of the Shadow Morph's hold. There's the barest sense of a scratch, but other than that, breaking loose was pretty easy.

I'd wonder about that but Jacoby is now standing before me with a curious look on his face.

Did he hear what I said about us not being bonded? Please don't let him have NOT heard A THING.

"We need to run," says Jacoby. "I've set a power orb to make set this place on fire."

"Fire yes." I smile so wide, my face hurts. "Let's go."

And I race out the door.

23

JACOBY

*A*gatha and I race outdoors. The moment our feet hit the sidewalk, my fire spell goes off. The glass windows of the coffee shop explode. Plumes of fire burst out into the street.

To protect Agatha from the blast, I curl my body around hers. We end up on the pavement with Agatha on her back under me. My hands are cupped behind her head. Heat and attraction burn through my veins.

"Are you all right?" I ask.

Agatha stares at my mouth a long time before answering. "You fried my coffee shop."

"Flame is the only way to fully kill a Shadow Morph."

"Oh." A deep blush colors her face. "I suppose we should get up now."

"Don't you want to stay and discuss how we got bonded?"

Agatha pounds my shoulder. "You heard! I knew you did."

I rise and offer Agatha my hand. "You were rather loud. It was hard to miss."

She stands up on her own. "Ugh. The Shadow Morph was talking in my head. Just forget it ever happened."

I can't. Not that I'll admit that to Agatha yet.

A high wail of sirens cuts through the night. "We can't hang around here for long." I step closer. "What do you want to do now?"

"You mean about…"

"All the unpleasantness, yes. A goo monster did try to attack you in a coffee shop."

"Well, I won't let someone drag me off to Nal'Adel's palace." She picks up her floppy hat from the street. The brim is torn off. "Aren't you going to say it isn't safe for me to stay in New York?"

"No."

"Why?"

"You're your own person, Agatha. You'll do as you wish. And if you want my advice, you'll ask for it."

A small smile rounds her mouth. "What I want is simple. I want my life back. Nal'Adel must stop hunting me. But for that, we need a plan… and a safe place to come up with one."

"In that case, the most secure spot to chat is my refuge."

"So you'll open another portal to Faerie?"

"Yes, but not here. Are you up for a short walk to Central Park?" I offer her my arm. Agatha only hugs her elbows more closely. So we stroll off side by side.

In the end, I decide that Agatha may not be taking my arm, but she is leaving New York for my home.

I consider that progress.

24

ELLE

*N*ot sure how long I tumble through the air, but I finally land. Fortunately, all the pizza I've been eating lately has my butt well padded for just such an occasion.

Who says double-cheese isn't good for you?

I brace my arms behind me and scope out the scene. I'm inside a closet. That can't be right. When Lady Cloake sent me tumbling through the ground, she said I was heading for the gemstone prison.

Even so, there's no denying reality. From where I'm sitting, There's nothing in this closet other than me, a clothing bar, and a few hangers.

And this is a gemstone prison? A closet?

Actually, I wouldn't put it past Nal'Adel. She seems like a mighty strange ranger. Who knows? Maybe she has thousands of enchanted closets hidden inside her magical rock.

It's so weird, it could just be brilliant.

The closet sports a single door. It's one of those tall numbers with wooden slats. Thin lines of light seep through the breaks in the wood. A large L-shaped handle gleams in the low light.

Huh. Getting out of here can't be *that* easy. Jacoby has told me all about elves. They're sneaky little shits of the first order. Elves are always doing stuff like camouflaging cliffs as comfy cabins—just so weary traveler will step through the front door and fall to their deaths.

So what does it mean that I'm inside a closet with an easy-looking exit? Nothing good.

Closing my eyes, I try reaching my inner magic. there's nothing. It's like knocking on an empty metal box. Which makes sense. If I were setting up a prison, I wouldn't allow anyone to cast spells.

Even so, I can't sit on the dusty floor forever. Inch by inch, I slowly rise to my full height. All the while, I keep on the lookout for tripwires or other boobytraps.

Nothing.

It takes a few minutes, but I'm soon standing at the wall with my fingertips resting on the metal handle.

I grip and turn.

The closet door swings open without a problem. Turns out, the room beyond is a dingy library. The gray wood walls hold shelves of leather-bound books. Cobwebs dangle from the ceiling. The air tastes like old cheese and new problems.

A guy stands with his back facing me. That said, I'd know him anywhere. My breath catches. Every cell in my body seems to go on edge.

"Alec?" I ask. "Is that you?"

The man turns around. My body feels watery with relief.

It *is* Alec.

Racing forward, I wrap him in a big hug. "I found you!"

Alec leans back and breaks the embrace. "I'm sorry. Do I know you?"

I roll my eyes. "Don't joke. It's me. Elle."

His eyes turn flinty and dark. "Most inmates here are subject to magical amnesia. I don't know who you are. Please do not touch me again."

Back when I was in the Old West, Lady Cloake had literally pulled the ground out from under me. If I thought that sensation threw me, it's nothing compared to what I'm feeling now.

Alec doesn't know me.

A minute ago, I suspected this place was filled with traps. Looks like I just stumbled across my first one.

GEMSTONE PRISON

25

ALEC

*I*t still doesn't seem real.

A minute ago, a lovely woman stepped out of the supply closet. When she wrapped me in a hug, it was beyond awesome. Unfortunately, this isn't the first time a pretty lady has stepped into the room and acted friendly. It's always ended in assassination attempts. I have a collection of daggers to prove it.

Even so, my latest visitor makes all the other beautiful faces pale into shadow. The girl carries herself like a blonde Amazon queen. Her blue eyes shine with an intelligence that's nothing less than hypnotic.

"You really don't know me," she whispers.

"That's something we can fix. Why don't you introduce yourself?"

This request has two purposes. First, I'm curious about her name. Second, her reply will tell me a lot about her true purpose here.

"Sure." She seems genuinely deflated. "I'm Elle."

I set my hands in my pockets. "I wish I could return the

favor and give you my name, but I'm afraid that's impossible. Like I told you before, I have magical amnesia."

"Your name is Alec." Her words hold a desperate edge.

The assassins who come into this room fall into one of two categories. The first kind know exactly who they are, what I am, and that it would please Nal'Adel to kill me. The second type are simply bat shit crazy. This girl seems to know her name, which would suggest she's the first type of assassin. Yet she also seems genuinely upset. Normally, that would put her in the second category.

So which is it? Is this woman a sophisticated assassin or a loony tunes prisoner? I must admit, the question is intriguing. This place is beyond gloomy. Figuring out this girl promises to be a fun distraction.

"Alec?" I turn the name over in my mind. "Doesn't feel right, to be honest. As a matter of fact, I've been calling myself Statler. I think it has quite a ring to it, don't you?"

Elle stares at me with her mouth slightly open. She doesn't seem thrilled by my choice.

"There's an extra benefit to the name Statler as well," I continue. "It's also the name of my favorite Muppet. Funny how amnesia works, eh? I remember characters from an old television show, yet I cannot recall my own name." I shrug. "Ah, well. Many folks here have it far worse. Their minds are trapped on a single thought from our captor, Nal'Adel."

Elle looks around the room. "So this is her prison?"

"Absolutely. This place is a magical representation of Nal'Adel's mind."

"Her what?"

"It takes a while to get used to this idea, but you are now part of a magical labyrinth of rooms that look like they belong in a haunted house. Some of those who are trapped here serve Nal'Adel. Others are her prisoners. We're essentially stuck inside Nal'Adel's unconscious mind."

"I get that this is her prison." Elle's gaze turns even more intense. "But why can I recall things while you can't?"

"Were you sent here by someone other than Nal'Adel?"

"Yes. Lady Cloake."

"Ah, then that explains it. I've met a few Lady Cloake additions to our little reality. She's not as powerful in magic as Nal'Adel. Your kind often arrive with your memories intact. Congratulations." I pull out a chair from the single desk in the room. "So. Tell me about me."

Chances are, this girl is just one sandwich short of a picnic. Still, I'm curious what kind of fantasy life she's dreamed up for me. Let's just say there's not much entertainment around here.

"You're Alec Le Charme, the CEO of the world's largest chain of jewelry stores."

I sniff. "That sounds like a bore. But now that I think upon it, Alec is a nice enough name. I'll answer to that, if you like."

The poor girl looks like I threatened her kittens. "Yes, I would like that."

At this point, any attempts at murders would have happened by now. Which raises a good question. "Do you plan to stay in this room?"

Elle frowns. "Where would I go?"

"Good question. How about I give you a little prison overview?"

"Sure."

"That's the door." I gesture toward the item in question. "Do not go through it. As I told you, this is an unusual prison.

The others in this place are not exactly *ready to play with others*. If the door opens—and anyone enters—be on your guard. Most folks here are either assassins or unhinged enough to kill."

Elle gives me the side-eye. "Am I supposed to take that as an insult?"

I must admit, she bounces back rather quickly. A minute ago, this woman was a puddle of sadness. Now, she's ready to take me on.

"Actually, you entered from the storage closet." Continuing with my flight-attendant style presentation, I wave toward that area in the room. "That's a new one. I've yet to determine what category you fall into."

The side-eye continues. "Thanks."

"The gemstone that we're trapped inside is rather rare. It's called an odelai. This very room is the nerve center of its magic. That's why we have a handy desk and chair combination." I knock on the desktop as evidence.

Elle's face is the definition of deadpan stare. "Wow."

"Agreed, the desk isn't the best. However, you're about to witness the finest part of this chamber. The books." I do a double-arm gesture to show off the shelves. "They contain Nal'Adel's thoughts."

Elle tilts her head. "Anything interesting?"

"Not really. The prison isn't set up to share anything useful. Still, I keep reading. One of these days, Nal'Adel is bound to slip up and blab something that could help me escape."

"How do you know so much about magical gemstones?"

I bob my brows. "Why don't you tell me?"

"I asked you first."

"Well, no one can counter that argument. I can't remember names, but I do recall how things work. Especially magical gemstones."

"That's because you're a wizard. As a matter of fact, you're the best wizard on earth."

"Oh. I like this version of my life. Anything else?"

"We're both part of the Magicorum. Our fairy tale is Cinderella. We both attended something called the Glass Slipper Ball."

I've actually heard about Cinderella templates, evil step-sisters, and Glass Slipper Balls from other visitors. This is the first time the conversation hasn't ended with a dagger being chucked in my direction.

"How did you end up here?" I ask.

"Agatha is my stepsister. Nal'Adel wants to kill her."

"Ah. If I only had a dime for every time a nice lady told me that in this room, I'd have at least seventy cents."

Elle shakes her head. "Do you believe *anything* I'm telling you?"

"Honestly? This place is a little bizarre—and the people here are just as zany—so I can't exactly trust your sanity right now. That said, this is the best conversation I've had in ages. Let's say, I'm willing to keep an open mind."

Elle hugs her elbows. "Okay, I can live with that." She steps over to a nearby bookshelf. "And these are Nal'Adels' thoughts?"

"Quite right, and they change daily. Nothing too interesting, though."

Elle flips a nearby book open. "This is all about how she wants to find the Queen of Moonbeams."

"That's a common theme in her work. Since I arrived, I've

spent quality time getting into Nal'Adel's head. It's a rather grim place, I'm afraid. She wishes to consume other people's magic. Their souls, you might say. It ends with their death. Rather gruesome stuff."

Snuffling sounds echo in from the outer hallway, followed by the drumroll of hooves hitting the floor.

Elle clutches the book against her chest. "What's that?"

"One of the other inmates. A minotaur. he comes through every day at this hour."

Crossing the room, I wait by the door. At the last possible second, I'll pull it open. If I don't, then the minotaur will charge through and busts everything into pieces. The prison is a self-healing spell, so it's not like I have to clean anything up. Still, I do worry about getting something in my eye one of these days.

Whoosh!

As I yank the door open, the minotaur charges through. He's a massive fellow in a loincloth and light upper body armor. His brown eyes look wild as he shouts the same thing as every other time he's visited.

"I must find the Vessel of Hours!"

Elle frowns. "Wait a second."

I wave her off. "Just stand back and let him go, otherwise he gets agitated and busts up the room."

Elle wags her finger at the minotaur. "I know you."

I stifle the urge to groan. *What a shame.* I've seen this before. Elle is confronting one of the less stable attackers in the prison. That's a sure sign of mental deterioration.

Poor girl. She won't last long.

26

ELLE

*a*lec goes on about how I shouldn't talk to the minotaur. I don't pay attention. He's been here too long. In my opinion, Alec is starting to lose it.

I step right in front of the minotaur. "You're part of Jacoby's herd." I snap my fingers, trying to recall more about the guy. "I have it. Your name is Xanthos."

"I must find the Vessel of Hours," repeats Xanthos. This time, his voice has less of a frantic edge to it.

I focus on Alec. "Finding the Vessel of Hours… that's a thought from Nal'Adel, right?"

"Correct," says Alec. "The search for the Vessel is pretty much the only concept in his brain."

"But Xanthos is part of Jacoby's herd. I have to know how he got here."

Xanthos scrapes at the floor with his right hoof. "I must find the Vessel of Hours!"

"No, your name is Xanthos. Let me prove it to you." I rub my neck and try to remember more. "Ah, I've got something else. You're the oldest member of his herd. You live on a ranch in Faerie."

Xanthos tilts his head. "I must find the Vessel of Hours?"

"You lead Jacoby's herd. There are mammoth bears, ice kelpies, and a will-o'-the-wisp swarm. Does that ring any bells?"

"No," says Xanthos.

I can't help but grin. Sure, Xanthos just said *no,* but at least he wasn't repeating, *I must find the Vessel of Hours.* If I keep pushing, I can get more out of him, I know it.

That's when my mental light bulb fires up in a big way.

"Jacoby told me all about your most favorite thing in the world. *Your momma* jokes."

"What?" Alec strikes one of his classic poses. By this, I mean that he sets his hands into his pockets while slightly tilting his head. The guy can't help it; he's always getting ready for someone's camera to go off. "Did you say *your momma* jokes?"

"That I did. Okay, Xanthos. Your momma's so fat, if she was a Star Wars character, her name would be Admiral Snackbar."

Xanthos holds his thumb and finger an inch apart. "That was a little bit funny."

I raise my voice. "Your momma's so old, when God said, 'Let there be light,' he shoved her out of the way."

Xanthos giggles. He has such a sweet-sounding laugh that I can't help but do one more.

"Your momma's so nasty, they used to call them jumpo-lines 'til she bounced on one."

Minotaur raises his hands. "I give up. You know me."

"Why are you here? You should be on Jacoby's land. You run his herd. They protect his refuge."

"Nal'Adel sent us all here," says Xanthos. "Jacoby is unprotected."

"You don't seem worried."

"Nal'Adel doesn't want to hurt Jacoby. She only wants to put Agatha through some ceremony."

"You talked about a Vessel of Hours. Is that what it's for? This ceremony?"

Xanthos nods. "It will help Nal'Adel drain Agatha's magic. But she needs something else as well. A rock."

That gets Alec interested. "You mean a magical stone?"

"Yes," agrees Xanthos. "A one-of-a-kind crystal."

"Do you know anything else?" I ask. "Where does this ceremony need to happen?"

"That's all I remember." Xanthos shivers and looks away. When his gaze meets mine again, his eyes are unfocused and glassy. "This is a library. How did I get here?"

"You always burst through the door at the same time every day," explains Alec. "It's how I keep track of time. So thanks for that."

"Where is the Vessel of Hours?" asks Xanthos.

My shoulders slump. "Xanthos? Do you remember your name?"

"I must find the Vessel of Hours!" Xanthos wanders off.

Alec turns to me. "That was amazing. I haven't seen anyone break through to another prisoner."

"Thanks, I guess."

"You still seem worried."

"Jacoby's property is his refuge. If someone got rid of his herd, then he's at risk" I press my palms against my eyes.

"What if Jacoby takes Agatha there to keep her safe? Then they are both walking into a trap." I drop my arms and step closer to Alec. "We need to look through the rest of the prison. Maybe there's someone else who can help."

Alec shakes his head. "This is the best room in the prison. It's the nerve center, so there's less traffic. If you go to other rooms, you spend all day fighting off one attack after another."

"But don't you think that's a little bit sketchy? Nal'Adel locks you in a prison and then tries to kill you?"

"*Sketchy* isn't quite accurate. *Obvious* is more the word I'd use. I'm stuck somewhere and everyone in the place is trying to kill me. But I've found a safe-ish room. Yay me. "

"You need to fight back."

"With what? I'm a gemstone wizard. Without any powerful stones, I'm walking into a trap. Can you cast spells?"

I shake my head. "I tried when I first got here. It didn't work."

"Precisely. So our best chance is to find Nal'Adel's weaknesses." Alec gestures across the wall. "Behold! Her every secret thought. Some are quite hilarious. Shall I read to you from the book of Nal'Adel's love life? It's got all of four words in it."

"Alec, please."

Alec opens a nearby book. "Here it is and I quote, *King Wyrran is hot.*"

I lean against the wall. "You'll be tough to convince."

"Try impossible. I must discover some sort of advantage that means I have an actual chance at life if I leave this room. My suggestion? Start reading. I haven't covered any of the shelves there." Alec gestures toward the opposite wall.

Cords of worry tighten around my throat. "Jacoby and Agatha are at risk. I can't just look at books."

"I disagree. Reading solves most problems, in my experience." Everything about him is so sweet and calm, I almost forget this isn't really *my* Alec.

"I'll give it a try," I say in a low voice.

After crossing the room, I pull a book from the shelves. Meanwhile, Alec stands at the other side of the chamber, searching through his own shelf of books.

Not too long ago, Alec and I read through a bunch of papers together. Our goal? Find out what was really happening at Le Charme Jewelers. We shared and sorted through every page, side by side. Now, we're on opposite ends of the room and Alec doesn't even remember who I am.

I've never felt more alone in my life.

27

ALEC

I hold my book high. Hopefully, I look as if I'm reading this list of Nal'Adel's favorite spells. In reality, I'm cheating glances in Elle's direction.

I still can't place her in the pattern of the prison. She's not a killer. Plus, it's clear that she's *more than sane*. The way Elle handled the situation with Xanthos was nothing less than brilliant.

Still, I can't lower my defenses. The whole point of this prison is to lull you into a sense of comfort... and then dig in with a knife. Nal'Adel wants this Agatha. I'm alive because somehow, I might be useful in helping her reach that goal. In my opinion, it's my gemstone wizard skills that Nal'Adel wants to exploit down the road.

That said, I'm not a crucial player. Nal'Adel is the kind of predator who likes to toy with a potential kill. Which is why I'm here. If I survive, I might be useful. Should I die? Well, I don't think I'm the most important captive in controlling or finding Agatha.

My mind whirls through Elle's claims. All this time, I

assumed Nal'Adel was keeping me alive so I could cast a spell or two. But what if I really am Elle's boyfriend? That might change everything. Elle claims that Agatha is her stepsister. If true, then I might prove helpful in a threat. *Give me what or I want or I'll kill Elle and Alec...* that kind of thing.

It's a long shot, but it's possible.

Yet when it comes to being a gemstone wizard, I have concrete proof of my skills. I know things, like how this place is built on an odelai stone. But Elle? There's nothing. Which is a shame. In this place, it would be wonderful to have a real connection to another human being.

Sighing, I return my focus to my own pile of books.

These volumes haven't served up anything useful yet. Still, I'll never give up. I won't spend an eternity hiding out in a screwy prison. At some point, Nal'Adel will make a mistake.

Then, I'll make my move.

CENTRAL PARK

JACOBY

I love strolling through New York at night. The place is always alive. Cars and pedestrians flow around at a steady pace. Plumes of mist erupt from the underground. The crisp edge of fall burrows under the late summer air.

And it's all better by having Agatha at my side. We're both quiet, but it isn't a tense silence. Agatha's the first to speak.

"Why didn't you open a portal outside Hyacinth?"

"That area isn't secure. The Shadow Morph must have been spent days inside the coffee shop, waiting for the command to strike. Who knows what other monsters are lurking nearby?"

Agatha nibbles her lower lip. "And Central Park is secure?"

"The Queen of Hearts rules that territory. And I happen to know that Nal'Adel's people aren't welcome there. If one of Nal'Adel's monsters sets foot on the grass, the red guard would be out in a heartbeat. We wouldn't need to fight alone."

"Clever," says Agatha.

"Thank you."

The pleasant silence between us returns. I soak in the friendly moments. This is what I should have been enjoying all along, instead of wondering if Agatha was lying to me.

Agatha breaks the quiet once more. "Could the Queen of Hearts keep me safe in New York?"

"Perhaps. You'd have to live on a Central Park bench, though." I purse my lips. "Which might be step up from the playroom."

Agatha shoots me the side-eye. "You're really afraid of those evil clowns, aren't you?"

"Guilty as charged." Pausing, I scan our surroundings. Agatha and I have been walking about the park for some time now. I was so focused on her, I didn't even notice. "Ready to travel?"

Agatha shivers. "Are you certain your refuge is safe?"

"It always *has* been." I step closer. "Yet I won't lie. I doubt anywhere is truly secure for you now."

Agatha pales. "I understand."

Accessing my inner magic, I summon an orb of power and open a door to faerie in the trunk of an obliging tree. A moment later, we step through onto the grounds of my personal refuge.

And the moment I stand on my land once more, I know one thing.

Danger is near.

JACOBY'S GARDEN

29

JACOBY

*P*ausing, I soak in every aspect of my home. Everything seems in place, including my cottage, fence, and gardens. A series of ward stones magically protect my grounds. I scan them all. None are broken.

Still, the skin on my neck prickles with worry. Anxiety swirls inside my nervous system.

What's wrong here?

I'm a Prince of the Fortitude, which means I wield magic over all things large and powerful. A herd of magical creatures guards my property. I must find Xanthos, the minotaur who cares for my herd. If anything is off, Xanthos will know what it is.

I jog to a nearby hilltop to find my herd sleeping on the fields below. I've never seen them so peaceful before.

Agatha calls from the nearby path. "Is everything alright?"

"Fine." I jog down the hill to stand at Agatha's side. "I needed to check on—" The rest of my words catch in my throat.

A minute ago, Agatha had turned pale as she worried if my

lands were safe. Now she looks positively deathly. This is something far more serious than regular worry.

"Agatha, are you all right?"

"Something's wrong." She blinks hard. "My arm."

I gently clasp her right wrist in my hands. With careful movements, I pull up her shirt sleeve. And black line marks her skin. My breath catches. "Did that Shadow Morph scratch you?"

"Sure." Agatha wobbles. "Only a little bit."

Stay calm, Jacoby.

Shadow Morphs are deadly. If their molten fingers break through the skin of a victim, then poison will slowly seep into their target's bloodstream. It takes a long time for real illness to set in. But once it does? The process is nearly impossible to stop.

How could I have been so stupid? Instead of checking Agatha for injuries, I was too concerned about getting her to safety. After that, I got so caught up in spending time together, I didn't consider anything else.

What if the poison has seriously infected her system? There's just one way to find out. I need to take a closer look at her arm. Little by little, I press up Agatha's sleeve. My heart sinks. A web of dark lines run up from the scratch mark and extend to her shoulder.

Oh, no. Agatha doesn't have much time.

There are some spells and antidotes in my cottage. The sooner I get Agatha there, the better chance she has to survive.

Scooping Agatha into my arms, I will my wings to appear as I fly off toward my cabin at top speed. One thought echoes through my soul.

Agatha, you have to live.

30

AGATHA

*M*y brain feels woozy. I try to focus on Jacoby, but the guy has transformed into a monster. As in, the man now has three separate heads. So confusing. Which face should I talk to? And why doesn't it bother me that two extra heads just showed up out of nowhere?

The dazed feeling moves from my head to my mouth. It's as if my lips are now on someone else's face. It isn't easy, but I manage to force out a few words. "Three heads."

Jacoby doesn't say anything in reply.

"You heads," I try to clarify.

Still no reaction.

At this point, I realize that I am moving through space at an amazing speed.

No, wait. That isn't it.

Jacoby has sprouted his wings again. Now I'm curled up in his arms while he flies us around.

This is way strange.

The good news is that Jacoby is back to having only one head again.

Total improvement.

JACOBY

$\mathcal{W}$ith all my focus, I will my wings to push harder through the night air. Agatha shakes gently as I clasp her against my chest. In this moment, it feels as If I hold everything precious and trustworthy in my arms.

I will save her. I have to.

My cottage is a rustic place with Tudor-style exterior of white plaster is framed by arches or dark wood. The contrast makes it easy to pick out in the dark.

As I close in, I focus on the ward stone by the front door. It's about the size of an ostrich egg. As I connect with its magic, the round stone glows with purple light.

When I swoop down, the ward stone does its job. The door swings open as I fly inside. The cottage interior is a lot of bare wood and wide spaces. This is so my herd can visit, but now it serves a better purpose. I'm able to soar down the hallway and land just outside Agatha's room.

Wait, when did I start thinking of the chamber that way? Agatha only stayed here briefly on her last visit. That said, she's the only visitor I've ever had. So there's that.

After setting Agatha down on the bed, I rush to my spell room and grab some quick supplies. Within minutes, I have my first serum ready. I pour one healing droplet on her lips.

Hiss! The liquid burns up when it touches her skin. that's the Shadow Morph magic, right there. It's enchanting any healing to self-destruct.

Yet no spell is perfect. Maybe some of the antidote got inside her. Grabbing a small knife, I slice open her right sleeve and check. Before my eyes, the black webwork of poison turns even darker.

A mixture of fear and rage heat my blood. That didn't work.

I return to my spell room and work up a new and more powerful tincture. All the while, I'm vaguely aware that I'm still showing my horns and wings. Even alone, I make it a habit to hide them. Now, I can't spare the magical energy.

With my next antidote, I try to give it to Agatha with enchanted tools. Hopefully, that will fight the burning affect of the Shadow Morph's magic. But the dropper melts. A syringe dissolves. Potions spray everywhere before they even near her mouth. In short order, I give up on shirts. It's easier to use them as towels.

Meanwhile, the webwork of poison spreads across Agatha's torso. Worry twists through my insides.

Next I place some antidote inside an orb of power and try to float it between her lips. The sphere becomes the worst splatter show yet.

By now, the dark lines now cover Agatha's arms and legs. Her breathing is shallow and rough. She doesn't have much longer.

Lacing my fingers behind my neck, I stare down at Agatha

and try to come up with a new plan. This can't be happening. How can I stand here and watch her die? There must be some way to give her the antidote that won't react with the Shadow Morph's magic.

I dip my finger in the serum and brush it across her lips. The antidote sizzles on my skin and burns.

That's when it hits me. There's a special kind of magic with real affection. Love. I must give it a try.

I brush more of the antidote across my lips. Then I lean over and press my mouth to hers. It's the gentlest of kisses. This time, nothing burns. My heart soars.

But did I give her enough antidote to do the job? I check Agatha's marks. The poison isn't spreading, but it isn't getting better, either.

I'm out of options. I've used every spell and tactic. I sit beside her on the bed. Words tumble from my lips.

"All those years growing up," I begin. "You don't think I saw you, but I did. I watched you read books in the back corner of the warehouse. You'd always purse your lips during the scary parts, and only lift one side of your mouth when things got funny. Your favorite backpack had a posey stitched on it. You only wore your purple floppy hat on Mondays."

Agatha takes in a long breath. It isn't a big sign. Still, that's the deepest breath she's taken in minutes.

"Please, Agatha. I know I didn't trust you before." I gently rub my fingers along her jawline. "So many of my brothers have been killed. That pain and loss blocked what my heart has really known for years. I love you, Agatha."

Before, the serum simply stayed on Agatha's mouth. Now it lights up with white magic. The lines of poison recede from her skin. She takes in a long series of breaths. Agatha opens her eyes and smiles.

I exhale. The antidote is working.

32

AGATHA

*E*very inch of my body feels on fire. Heat prickles on my arms. Foul tastes erupt in my mouth. Flares of light shine in my peripheral vision.

A cool cloth touches my forehead. The sense that my skin is burning fades away.

I open my eyes a crack and force out a few words. "So cold."

Jacoby now pats that chilly cloth down my arms. "Your fever just broke. It's a good thing."

I croak out another word. "What?"

"I'll explain everything later," says Jacoby. "For now, you need to sleep."

So that's what I do.

And I dream about Jacoby.

Normally, the prince is careful to hide his wings and horns. Yet in my dreams, he stands beside my bed with all his secret elfy stuff on display. And he's also not wearing a shirt either for some reason.

Major bonus.

JACOBY

33

AGATHA

Opening my eyes, I find myself in bed. And not just anywhere, but in Jacoby's cottage. I remember this room from my last visit. I blink hard, trying to remember how I got here in the first place. I recall Jacoby opening a portal to his cottage. But after that, everything gets fuzzy.

Turning over, I find Jacoby is standing beside the bed. He's all things bare-chested and fierce. A girl could find worse ways to wake up.

A speech begins without any specific planning from my head. I blame the bare-chested thing. "I dreamed about you last night."

Jacoby chuckles. "That happens a lot when you're me."

"I saw you standing by my bed with wings and horns showing. I thought that was just a dream."

"It wasn't. Last night, I couldn't cast glamours to hide my true form and save your life at the same time. Afterward, I kept up a vigil to ensure you're recovering. Guess the glamours slipped my mind."

My heart lurches in my chest. *Jacoby saved me?*

"Oh."

A small smile rounds Jacoby's mouth. He fixes me with a look that I can only describe as overwhelming. My stomach feels as if it's spinning about, pinwheel-style. The moment turns too intense.

Better change the subject.

I try to force myself to sit up, but it isn't easy. Jacoby helps me and fluffs a few pillows along the way. Once I'm in place, I try sorting through everything that happened. I pull up my sleeve. "What got me sick… Was it that scratch from the shadow morph?"

"Yes, it put poison in your system."

"I also dreamed you had something on your chin… or mouth, maybe?"

Jacoby raises his brows. "You remember that?"

"Sure."

"I couldn't get the antidote into you. I cast spells. Poured infusions. Tried injections. Nothing would take until I put some of the antidote on my lips and…"

I picture kissing Jacoby. The very thought does all sorts of strange things to my insides.

Huh. Maybe I heard him wrong.

"You kissed me?" I ask.

"For medicinal purposes only."

"Oh."

I focus on Jacoby's lips. His mouth is full and firm. What would it be like to kiss him while I'm awake? The idea sends waves of warmth and attraction running through me. Looking up, I meet Jacoby's gaze. A fire lights his eyes.

And a beam of light shines through my comforter. It's coming from my hip.

A memory appears. I felt this way when Jacoby and I were swimming in Sweetwater Cove. My moonbeam mark started glowing back then, too.

Grabbing a pillow, I set it over the spot. "This is awkward."

"I don't see why. Many elves have magical tattoos. Where did you get yours?"

"I was born with it."

"Really?" Jacoby steps closer. "May I see your mark?"

"You didn't check it last night?"

"No, I was more concerned with other things."

I blush. "Oh." *I seem to be saying that a lot today.*

Bit by bit, I pull the comforter aside, revealing the image of a crescent moon with three stars. The mark glows on my skin, along with some odd words that Jacoby traces with his fingertip. Everywhere the prince touches me, there's a trail of electric excitement on my skin.

"It's the most beautiful thing I've ever seen," he says, his voice husky.

A bubble of awareness forms around us. The rest of the world seems to vanish. "Can you read the words?"

Jacoby nods.

"What do they say? Tell me."

"I can't. That's your true name, Agatha. If I say it aloud..." He lets the logic hang out there.

We'd become bonded.

Yet again, I can only manage a single word. "Oh."

A rhythmic thud echoes in from outside the windows, breaking up the moment. I can't decide if that makes me happy or depressed.

"What's that noise?" I ask.

"It's probably Xanthos. He normally checks in during the morning."

Jacoby crosses the room to look out the window. His mouth thins to a worried line.

"What is it?" I ask.

"Trouble." Jacoby's stance turns straight and tall. Suddenly, he's all princely again. "You know how Nal'Adel is the Queen of Moonshadow, which is the opposite of Moonbeams? I'm the Prince of Fortitude, and my opposite is the Miniscule. We don't play well together. One of their representatives is on the way. His name is Froth and he's top counselor to their leader, Kaiser Mandrake."

"How can you be sure?"

"All Miniscule wear plague masks. And Froth's version is rather dark and pointy. He also carries a particular walking stick."

My eyes widen. "Plague?"

"Don't worry. They only release disease if they think they can get away with it. And with me, they won't try."

Even so, something in his face tells me that Jacoby isn't so sure of what he just said.

FROTH

34

JACOBY

*A*fter changing into more formal clothes, I step into my main reception chamber. It's a long and rectangular space made of wood. A line of benches surrounds the walls. I smooth the folds of my tunic and wait for the inevitable. Sure enough, it happens.

Low knocks sound at the main door. I pause and count to twenty before answering. It wouldn't be good to seem overly interested here.

I pull the door open. Froth stands on the cobblestone path outside. He's a squat figure in his black cloak. The pointed face of his plague mask gleams in the morning sun. He leans against his cane.

"Hello, Prince Jacoby." Under that cloak, Froth is not a unified being as most fae are. Instead, he's a conglomeration of countless tiny particles. All of which is why when he speaks, Froth sounds like a thousand low voices whispering at once.

"Greetings, Froth." Turning, I march into my home.

I don't bother inviting him inside. Froth knows to follow

me into the chamber. Once we're both inside, Froth gets right to business.

"I am here for one simple reason," says Froth. "Your herd is gone. Your power is nil."

Over the years, I've learned to carefully school my features. For a fraction of a second, my eyes widen in surprise. I quickly restore my look of calm detachment, but it's too late.

Froth can tell that his accusation has caught me unaware. Normally, my spies give me a heads-up on any rumors about my supposed weakness.

But can Froth be right? Is my herd really gone?

The moment I stepped through the portal, I knew something was wrong. Normally, I would have gone to check on my herd at close range. But they seemed so peaceful, I didn't want to bother them. Then Agatha fell ill. Whatever worried I may still have held got pressed to the back of my mind as I focused on healing her... and then watching her recover.

I turn the idea over in my mind. It isn't possible for my entire herd to have vanished. That would require more power than I've ever seen in Faerie. Which leaves one option.

"You're lying," I state.

"Cast a spell," retorts Froth. "Prove me wrong."

My muscles tighten with shock. For the first time, I consider the fact that my herd may actually be stolen away.

I simply must know the truth.

Magic swirls inside me all the time. I now pull on that energy and focus it before me. An orb of power materializes between my palms. I speak an order in my mind.

Show me my herd.

Different images appear inside the sphere. There are the rolling fields where my main herd lives. The caves that house my two-headed bears. The barn which my harpies call home. All are empty.

My herd is gone.

That can only mean one thing. When I checked my fields last night, there must have been some kind of illusion set over the place.

Damn. Again, I thought they all looked too peaceful. I should have suspected magic was at work.

Lowering my arms, I dismiss the spell. In this moment, I wish Froth had an actual face instead of a mask. That way, I could read his features. Without seeing any expressions, I must run through the logic of the situation. The smart money is on the fact that Kaiser Mandrake has somehow kidnapped my herd and now wants a ransom.

"Why are you here?" I ask.

"It isn't what I wish, but what my master requires. He knows you're a clever fellow. He asked me to stop and inspect the situation."

I spin his words through my mind. *Inspect the situation.* Kaiser Mandrake sent Froth over here to find out if I'm unprotected. Which I am.

"And what are you looking for in particular?"

"You have quite the collection of healing herbs and magical items. My master finds such things interesting." Froth steps closer. "What's to stop me from taking these items from you right now?"

So that's the true meaning for Froth's visit today. Someone else took my herd. Considering who's sleeping in my guest room, I'm now guessing that evildoer to be none other than

Nal'Adel. Froth isn't here to request ransom. He's more of an early vulture come to pick over the carcass of my property.

I inspect the air around Froth's body. His form is surrounded by what look like dust motes. They aren't. These are some of the particles that make up Froth's consciousness. I've seen this happen before. Froth is prepping little bits of himself to fly away and alert others from the Miniscule.

Kaiser Mandrake has a limited number of battle tactics. One of his classics is to send in a minion as scout before releasing his entire army. What Mandrake lacks in creativity he more than makes up for in effectiveness.

"How many of your brethren are lurking by my borders?" I ask.

"Two hundred and seventy-three."

In other words, a good part of Mandrake's army. Now if I had my herd here, I could simply summon up one of my sky whales. They skim particles from the air just as their counterparts siphon krill from the water. All of the Kaiser's army would be consumed in minutes.

But my sky whales are gone. Froth is right.

I'm unprotected and alone.

Even worse, so is Agatha.

35

AGATHA

*A*s I lie in bed, I can't help but overhear Jacoby and Froth. I'm no expert in politics, but it's pretty clear that this Minuscule person is here to cause trouble. And an army of plague guys are lurking nearby.

Think, Agatha. There must be something I can do.

A plan forms. Sure, it involves joining Jacoby and Froth, which won't be easy.

It's certainly possible, though.

I force myself out of bed, open Jacoby's dresser, and pull out one of his fancier tunics. The thing is covered in jewels that are made to look like tiny bulls. Must be for fancy occasions. Perfect.

Raising my arms, I slip it over my head. It looks like I'm wearing a potato sack, which is my normal look. However in this case, I must resemble a queen. So I fish around a little more and find a belt. I tie it up and give a little more *fancy* to my *pants.* With the belt in place, I kick off my shoes and go for the *barefoot fae look.* None of Jacoby's shoes fit me, so this will have to do.

With slow steps, I saunter into Jacoby's main reception chamber. At least, I hope it looks like a saunter. Truth is, I feel so sick I can only go super slowly. Even so, I've seen Ivy and Marchesa work this walk often enough.

I can pull it off. Possibly.

My legs feel like wet noodles below me. With every passing second, my gait gets more unsteady. When I finally reach the main room, I have to lean against the doorjamb to stop myself from falling over. Jacoby's back is to me. There's no missing the tightness in his shoulders. The prince is worried.

For his part, Froth's angles his mask toward me. "Agatha."

Jacoby turns around. The moment he sees me in the doorway, his features fall slack with shock and worry. He points toward my bedroom. No question what he'll say next. *I should be resting.*

Which is true.

It's not going to happen, though.

I try to lift my hand in a queenly gesture, but my arm feels too weak to do more than twitch. I raise my chin instead. "I am Queen Kir'Adel of Moonbeams." That seems a little short in terms of titles, so I add on a little more. "You look upon a revered ally to the Seelie Court."

That's a lot for Froth to process. If you asked me, the fact that I exist should be a major shock. That's not what Froth focuses on, though.

"The Seelie court," Froth repeats.

I know enough about politics to realize that all this focus on the Seelie court means something. Sadly, I'm too out of it to process what that might be.

Fortunately, Jacoby does.

A satisfied gleam shines in the prince's eyes. Seconds ago, Jacoby was all slack with worry. Now the lines of his face tighten into an expression of detached amusement. I don't know what's going on, but I'm glad Jacoby is on top of things.

Oh, no. My legs decide that now is a great time to turn extra noodle-like. It's only a matter of seconds before I face-plant into the floor.

The prince rushes to my side and wraps his arm around my waist. "Your Highness, you should be seated. That's the only appropriate stance for one of your station."

I couldn't walk if I wanted to, but Jacoby is able to slide me onto a nearby bench. Somehow I manage to speak with a steady voice. "Thank you."

Jacoby takes sits down beside me. Thankfully, he maintains his grip on my shoulders. If he didn't, I'd probably fall over.

Froth steps closer. It's hard to tell what the guy is looking at, considering how he's just a pointy face and a cape. But the eye holes of his mask reflect the image of Jacoby's hand on my shoulder.

Like my mention of the Seelie court, that feels important. But just like that previous hint, I don't have the mind power to process what it means right now.

"You're a bonded pair?" asks Froth.

Ah, so that's what he's thinking. I hadn't considered pushing this angle, but it makes sense. My plan didn't go farther than showing up and throwing around my status as Queen of the Moonbeam court. But if I'm bonded with Jacoby? That's definitely a replacement for his missing herd.

I couldn't have set things up better myself. If Froth thinks that Jacoby and I are bonded and can share power, then he won't release the Mandrake's army.

"Are we a bonded pair?" I repeat. "Of course."

Froth steps closer. "Yet you don't smell like a bonded pair."

There are two key things here. I had no idea getting bonded made you give off a unique scent. Plus, who knew that this guy could smell anything through a mask?

Jacoby gently kisses my cheek. "How right you are, my love." He glares at Froth. "Do not doubt my Queen."

My mind takes a snapshot of the moment. Sure, this is a terrible situation. Hundreds of plague monsters are waiting nearby, ready to swoop in and do who-knows-what to me and Jacoby. Even if I could wield my magic, I'm way too tired to take on an army. And Jacoby isn't at his best either, considering how he drained his magical reserves to keep me alive.

Yet even with all this? I love the feeling of him kissing my cheek.

A chill runs down my back. Did I just think the word *love*? I must be more ill than I thought.

Froth walks closer. "You look unwell, your Majesty."

I gasp. "Did I tell you to come closer to my royal person? I did not."

Froth steps backward. "If you're so healthy and powerful, then you'll be able to visit Kaiser Mandrake tomorrow evening. I'm sure he would very much like to congratulate you two on your bonding."

I sigh. "That sounds rather boring." I look to Jacoby. "Don't we have more important things to do?"

In all truth, I'd rather have a tooth pulled than go see Kaiser Mandrake. But Jacoby knows the politics here far better than I do. If he thinks we need to trot past the kingpin plague doctor in order to prove we're really a team, then I can rally.

Jacoby waves his hand dismissively. "I suppose we can stop by Lilliput tomorrow evening." He glares at Froth. "If you leave right now, that is."

"Of course." Froth bows to me and Jacoby in turn. Finally, he walks away.

The moment the door closes, I slump against Jacoby's shoulder. "That sucked."

"I disagree." The prince kisses the top of my head. "That was one of the most brilliant shows of political acumen I've ever seen. What an achievement, Agatha. Is there some kind of prize I can award you?"

"How about some chicken soup?"

"Consider it done."

36

JACOBY

*S*cooping Agatha into my arms, I carry her back to her room. Once she's settled in place, I conjure up some chicken soup. I'm pretty drained from last night, but one bowl isn't too much.

Agatha takes a cautious sip. "It's delicious."

"There's a human television show with a so-called Soup Nazi. Turns out, it's a fae who runs a real place in midtown manhattan. He taught me the recipe and I can summon up it up at will."

"It's a perfect reward." Agatha finishes half the bowl and leans back onto her pillow pile. She tries to focus on me. Her eyes flutter to stay open.

I pull the bowl from her hands. "Perhaps you can finish the rest later on." I start to leave, then pause. "So you know, I won't hold you to visiting Kaiser Mandrake. I can make up a plausible excuse. What do you want to do?"

Agatha's eyes are only open the barest amount. "Don't you think the question should be, what do *we* want to do? It looks like we're a team."

My heart warms. "I didn't want to assume."

"What I want to do is live in New York and fix up Cynder Mercantile. But this thing with Nal'Adel just hit the next level. It's become more than finding a Vessel and Eye in order to bring back the Seelie imperials. Nal'Adel took your herd, Jacoby. I liked all of those folks and I want to take the fight to her." She fully closes her eyes. "But for now, I need to rest."

"Sweet dreams," I say. And if some extra innuendo gets in my voice, so be it. I know Agatha pictures me mostly naked last night. Does she remember as well?

In reply, Agatha blushes a deep shade of red. Oh, she recalls everything, all right. As I leave the room, I take that as a very good sign indeed. Agatha and I are rebuilding here. I won't give up until what we said today is the truth.

Agatha and I are bonded.

With that happy thought in mind, I step down the hallway toward the main room. A view out my window stops me in my tracks.

Froth lied.

There's no plan to host me and Agatha at Lilliput. I know this because the plague army now hovers outside my window.

Damn.

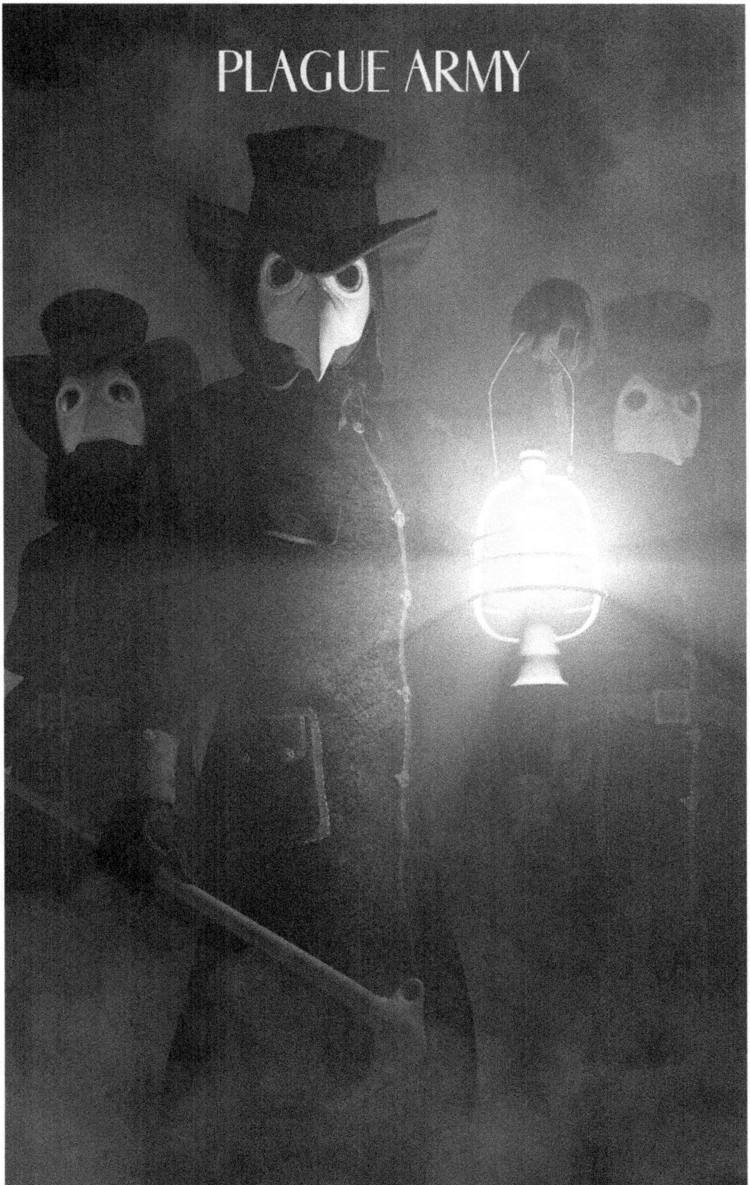
PLAGUE ARMY

37

JACOBY

*W*aves of shock careen through my nervous system. Hundreds of plague doctors wait outside my cottage.

Clearly, Froth didn't believe Agatha and I were together. Instead, he saw that it was only a matter of time before we actually did become bonded.

And decided that now is the best time to strike.

Outside the window, the many warriors dissolve into a miasma of small black particles. Those tiny bits of disease seep into the cottage through countless crevices and openings.

Under the door.

Around the windowsill.

Through slats in the ceiling.

Within seconds, I'm surrounded by a dark cloud. You don't grow up as the opposite to the Minuscule without knowing what each hue of their attack clouds represents. And this particular color? Sleeping sickness.

Curse the luck. If I were at full strength, I could cast some protection orbs to keep the Minuscule away. As it is, I can only rush toward Agatha's room. By the time I reach the threshold, the air is already thick with miasma.

While I've been gone, Agatha has somehow forced herself to stand. When she sees me enter the chamber, she reaches toward me. "What's happening?"

I try to walk closer, but my legs feel as if they're filled with cement. My ability to speak seems to be weighed down as well. It's an effort to force out a two-word reply.

"Sleeping... sickness."

White spots appear before my vision. I battle against the illness, but it's no use. My consciousness fades.

I pass out.

GEMSTONE PRISON

38

ELLE

*D*ays pass slowly when you're trapped in the world's weirdest prison. And that's if we're even on the same time cycle as the rest of the universe, which I suspect we're not. On the plus side, we don't need to eat, drink or go to the bathroom.

But that's also a bit of a negative as well. Doing those things helps to pass the time. Instead, I read books, chat with Alec and wait for Xanthos to run through.

Normally, Alec and I can blab about nothing for hours. This version of my boyfriend acts like I'm about to pull a knife on him any second.

Then I find his dagger collection. Turns out, a bunch of other chicks did pull weapons on him.

So that explains a lot.

I kill the hours by reading books crammed with odd trivia about Nal'Adel. Here are some of what I've learned. Nal'Adel hates broccoli, likes hair styling gel, and wants power. Whenever I run across an interesting tidbit, I try to share it with Alec.

For his part, Alec always replies and grins. But I know the guy. He's totally humoring me.

Not gonna lie. It hurts.

Outside of reading, my other entertainment is watching the array of monsters and oddballs that walk past the exit door. Not that I'm crazy enough to actually leave the library. But it's interesting to watch who creeps past the window.

Take today, for instance. So far, I've seen a stone giant, two kelpies and a three-headed harpy. Some of these folks must be from Jacoby's herd. But I know for a fact that Jacoby doesn't like stone giants.

So Nal'Adel has been a busy little lady.

I've spent my morning reading another book from my least favorite elf queen. This one covers the best ways to either clean castle tapestries or disembowel your enemies. Turns out, these are two of her favorite things to do.

This chick is so evil, I can't even.

Then I see it.

Idjit the troll walks by the library door. Total shocker.

I know this guy because he's the personal chauffeur for none other than Colonel Mallory the Magnificent. It was Idjit who drove me, Bry, Knox, and Alec to the pyramids of Egypt. Idjit even saw us release tons of magic into the atmosphere.

And now the guy is in Nal'Adel's prison? Whoa.

I point at the window. "Do you see that guy?"

Alec acts super interested in his book. "Did you say something?"

I roll my eyes. "It's a small room and there are only the two of us. Of course, I said something and to you." I gesture toward the window. "Check out this troll. Tell me if he looks familiar to you."

Alec saunters across the room and stares through the door. "That fellow *does* look familiar."

"Come on." I tug on his elbow. "Let's go talk to him."

"Not a chance. There are assassins loose in this prison. They have one target."

"Fine. You stay here. I'm going."

Alec moves to stand directly in my way. "No. It's isn't safe."

"Please. Don't make me hurt you." I go up on tiptoe, which is a bad idea, considering how our mouths are now level with each other. "You've no idea what I can do."

Alec grins. "You know what? I think you might just be right." He steps aside. "Lead on, Milady."

"You're going *with* me?"

"It seems that when we're together, I don't feel quite as... what's the right word?"

"Chicken shit?"

"That works."

"Knox always said you worked best as a team."

Alec tilts his head. "Knox?"

"Your best friend who also happens to be dating my best friend. And they're both off an adventure with Colonel Mallory the Magnificent. Spoiler alert—this troll is the Colonels' personal driver."

Alec looks at me and glances away. I point right at his nose. "I know that look, by the way. You know something that you think will upset me and you're debating whether or not to come clean." I don't mean to, but I lean in even closer to his mouth. "If we're a team, it's best if we really share."

Alec stares at my mouth for a moment before speaking. "One of the books here talked about Knox and Bry. Their so-called adventure to find out what happened to the missing magic? It's really a wild goose chase. The only real purpose to their travels is to keep them away from both Faerie and Agatha."

I nod slowly and process this news. "That sucks, but it makes sense. Because if Bry, Knox, and the Colonel knew what was going on here? There would be no end to the ass kicking."

Alec gives me a shy smile. "They sound like good friends. I can't wait to meet them. Again."

"We will." But those two words come out with a lot less confidence than I'd like. After all, we're about to step out into the prison labyrinth with nothing but my big mouth and Alec's smile to protect us.

With any luck, that will be enough.

FIDJIT

39

ALEC

*E*lle steps out into the next room in line. It looks exactly like the library, only there are no books. But there is an evil hipster troll.

Damn, does that guy ever look familiar.

Elle waves at the guy. "Hey, Idjit."

The troll stares guiltily at his hands "That's my twin brother. I'm Fidjit."

I eye the guy carefully. "And why are *you* here?"

"Lady Cloake sent me to kill you both." He grins, showing off a mouth of needle-like teeth.

"Which you could do," says Elle smoothly. "But then Colonel Mallory would find you and chop you up into little troll bits."

I've seen this attitude before from Elle. What some folks do with swords, she does with words. *Brilliant.*

"Once you kill us, do you know how to exit this prison?" I ask.

Fidgit frowns. "No."

That's a total lie. This guy absolutely has an escape plan. Elle and I just need to find out what it is.

"Come on," says Elle. "If you let Alec and I loose, there must be something you want in return. You know, other than not getting killed by the Colonel."

Fidjit raises his hand. A flash of light appears on his palm. When the brightness vanishes, a round crystal is gripped in Fidget's fingers. "I want nothing less than the Eye of the World."

The gemstone is unmistakable. "That's another kind of odelai," I announce. "Those are exceptionally rare."

"How about this?" asks elle. "We'll get you a magical ruby from Le Charme Jewelers. That's what your help is worth."

It's official. I'm starting to really like Elle.

"I want three rubies," snaps Fidjit.

Elle shakes her head. "I don't know." She looks to me. "What do you say?"

"I suppose I could find three." If I really run a jewelry store, that shouldn't be too hard. I offer Fidjit my hand. "It's a deal." We shake on the bargain. "Now, how do we escape?"

"Travel four rooms to the right, three to the left, and then open the closet. After that, kick through the wall. That will take you to a special chamber which acts as the border between this stone and reality. Easy peasy."

A weight of worry seeps from my shoulders. After so many days of being trapped in this prison, I might actually be leaving.

"See you later, oh friends of Colonel Mallory." The troll starts to speed walk in the opposite direction.

Elle raises her hand. "One last thing."

I lift my right brow. Before today, I might have worried about what Elle's up to. But now?

I can't wait to see what she'll come up with next.

40

ELLE

I don't trust this troll. He's been acting guilty as hell since we walked through the door. I leap to stand between him and the exit.

"One question for you. How did you get mixed up with Nal'Adel?"

Fidget hops from foot to foot. Now I can see where he got his name. "I didn't tell Nal'Adel anything."

Alec and I share a long look. I'm the first to speak. "Are you thinking what I'm thinking?" I ask Alec.

"Oh, yes," he replies.

I look to Fidjit. "Let me fill in a few blanks here. Your brother trusted you with some information, like how we released magic into the ether. And you sold that info to Nal'Adel."

Fidjit twists his hands and stares up at the ceiling. "Maybe."

Now, I can tell when I'm working with a chatty criminal. Fidjit is what I like to call a Super Blabber. Basically, he talks and talks until he finds something he can do or sell for treasure.

My kind of guy.

"Come on, Fidjit," I urge. "Spill."

Fidjit purses his lips. "If I tell you, what's in it for me?"

"Three magical rubies," I offer. "We can do that, right Alec?"

"Absolutely," lies Alec. "Just need a few weeks to get our stock together." Alec offers his hand to Fidjit. The two of them shake on the bargain.

"Back to spilling," I order.

"Nal'Adel can see the future," explains Fidjit. "She knew the Seelie imperials could be raised and drained soon. By the time I met her, she's already acquired the Vessel of Hours. But she couldn't find the Eye of the World."

"Which is why you wanted to see if we had it," suggests Alec.

"Exactly," confirms Fidjit. "Nal'Adel had been looking for the Eye of the World in tombs and treasure hoards. I sold her information about how my brother helped bring magic back into the world, and I think it put her on the right path."

I frown. "Well, that's not too helpful."

"I think I know what he means," says Alec. "Magic getting released into the atmosphere meant that a new gemstone could be created somewhere." Alec's eyes widen. "It explains how Nal'Adel got her hands on such a rare rock to create this prison in the first place. This odelai is newly-grown."

I don't want to look like a dumb ass here, so I nod quietly as if everyone knows how magical gemstones grow in new places.

"So that explains how you got involved with Nal'Adel," I

state. "Why are you here to kill us now?" My eyes widen as the truth hits me. "It's Agatha. Nal'Adel was keeping us here in case she needed our help to find my stepsister. That evil queen has Agatha, doesn't she?"

Fidjit shrugs at stares at the floor. "Yes. If I tell you what Nal'Adel plans to do with your sister, will you give me three more rubies?"

"Yes, agreed," I say quickly.

Fidjit grins. The guy really has disgusting needle-teeth. "Here's what I know," begins the troll. "Agatha is some kind of chosen girl. She's the only person who can put the Eye of the World into a bowl called the Vessel of Hours. When that happens, some of the Seelie imperial family will return. Only Nal'Adel doesn't want any of those elves back. She wants to take their magical energy, kill them and become the ultimate Empress of Faerie. How about that, eh? Really, all that info is a bargain for three rubies."

I take a half-step backward. My limbs turn numb with shock. Fidjit's not kidding. That's a ton of news. Seelie elves returning? Agatha is a chosen one? Nal'Adel wants to take over Faerie? I'd gotten pieces of this story before, but not the whole picture.

And what an ugly image it is.

Fidjit cups his hand, then huffs a breath over his very long nails. "That's all I've got to sell to you. Now, if you don't mind, I've other business in this prison."

With that, Fidjit runs away.

At this point, I'm feeling too numb to think through the fact that Fidjit is racing off. I look toward Alec. "Should we go after him?"

Alec bobs his head for a few moments before answering. "No, I think he's really given us all the secrets that he can sell."

I pace a line inside the chamber and try to gather my thoughts. All this new information only means that Agatha's in more danger than I thought. I round on Alec. "We need to get out of here and find Agatha. Fast."

"Agreed."

I tilt my head. "But you don't remember Agatha. If you don't know her, why would you want to help me?"

Alec gives me one of his thousand-watt smiles. "Well, I am a member of the world, and it looks like Nal'Adel wants to rule it. Plus, it's like you said. The pair of us can accomplish amazing things together. I'd like to see where that goes."

I can't help but grin. "I didn't really say that, but I like the way you talk, mister."

And we take off in the opposite direction.

ALEC

*W*e follow Fidjit's instructions. Shockingly enough, the troll told the truth. Don't get me wrong; it's not like I want Fidjit at my next birthday dinner. But it does seem as if the guy deserves his magical rubies.

Elle and I speed through four rooms to the right, three to the left, and then open the closet. Along the way, we run across a Norse fighting squirrel and two ghosts, but nothing major. Nal'Adel must have cleared this path for Fidjit to leave the prison once he finished his task.

Each room looks the same as the library: dark, creepy, and covered in dust. Once we reach the final chamber, Elle does the honors of kicking through the wall. As Fidjit promised, beyond that barrier there's a large and modern-style room made from stacked blocks of onyx. An octagon-shaped pit sits in the center of the floor. The shape reminds me of the top facet of a gemstone.

This is the exit; I know it.

The chamber pulses around me. The square blocks shift

back and forth in waves. I gesture toward a nearby wall. "Do you see that?"

Elle shakes her head. "This looks like a black stone room to me." She narrows her eyes. "How does it appear to you?"

"It's moving."

"Oh, this is definitely your magic."

"How so?"

Elle steps closer. "Think about it. So much is happening right now. Agatha has just come out of hiding as an elf, there are at least two super-rare odelai crystals loose in the world, and the Seelie may rise again... why would all of this happen now?"

I set my hands in my pockets and try to follow her train of logic. "You're talking about that trip to the pyramids."

"Yes, we released tons of magic into the world. You did too. And your magic is gemstone power. What if those two odelai stones are *yours,* meaning that they grew from the magic you released? This prison directed you to the only room that can keep you safe. No one else was there. And now this place actually moves for you. It must be *your* magic."

"There's more." I close my eyes. "In this room, I can hear voices, too. There are men, women, and children. I can't make out anything they say, but their tones are beautiful."

"This is definitely your power returning." She steps up to the edge of the hexagon-shaped pit. "Wherever this pit leads, it's part of you and your powers."

I eye her carefully. At one point, I suspected that Elle was unhinged. I search inside myself, wondering if that assessment is still there. It isn't. There's no doubt about it.

I believe Elle. I trust her.

And the implications of that are huge. Maybe I am her

boyfriend. Perhaps I really serve as the warden of wizard magic. I might have a full and beautiful life waiting for me.

All of a sudden, I don't want to leave this prison just because the place is awful. I want to go so I can regain my true self. Even though we've only been together for a few days, I'm already starting to fall for Elle. I want more.

So I move to stand beside Elle. "Let's jump."

"On the count of three?"

"1, 2, 3!"

With that, we clasp hands and leap off into the darkness. A moment later, we land in a cave.

Before, Elle said that the prison stone had been created with my own power. But my connection to the prison is nothing compared to what I sense here.

Because this place is more than a cave. It's a nursery for magical stones.

NURSERY

42

ALEC

*A*t first, Elle and I are only surrounded by silence and darkness.

Then a single rock illuminates nearby. Blue light pulses within the stone. Next a trio of rocks become bright as well. Soon glowing crystals stretch out into the darkness. There must be hundreds of them.

The voices return, only far more loudly. I can even make out words this time.

Seelie

Imperial

Eone

All around us, the crystals pulse with light once more. Then actual images appear inside the stones. My breath catches. This is rare magic indeed.

I step closer to one of the larger rocks. Inside, there's a

lovely elf in a green gown. Jewels dangle from her pointed ears.

Elle moves over to another crystal. "Do you see these people?"

"Yes, and I hear them talking as well. They're Seelie imperials from the old empire. They say Eone preserved them inside these crystals."

Elle nods. "Fidjit talked about the Seelie Imperial court being brought back."

I press my hand against one of the crystals. The stone pulses with life. "We need to find Agatha, the Eye of the World, and the Vessel of Hours... fast. Otherwise, Nal'Adel will hurt all these people."

"Can you use any of these gemstones to find Agatha? Wherever she is, I bet we'll find the Eye and Vessel, too."

I shake my head. "I can't break off any of these stones to use for my own magic. And we shouldn't cast any spells inside the caves, either. It could ruin the enchantment that protects these elves."

"The Eye and Vessel can't be far," announces Elle. "After all, they're meant to somehow bring back these folks. Spells work best with proximity." She points to one of the darkened archways leading out from the cavern. "Maybe we just get out of here the old fashioned way?"

I rub my chin, considering. "Whatever this spell may be with the Eye and Vessel, it must be cast above ground or close to it. We should try the far-right exit. The ground slopes upward there, which should bring us to the surface faster."

"Far right it is," says Elle.

And we take off at a run.

DUNGEONS

43

AGATHA

The last thing I remember, strange smoke was filling up my bedroom. Then I reached for Jacoby.

And everything went dark.

Now, I open my eyes and find myself lying on a cold stone floor. The place is black as midnight. Condensation drips down the rock walls. A line of bars looms before me. On the other side of the barrier, there's Jacoby. The prince does not look well. Jacoby's skin is pale. Dark circles hang under his eyes.

"Agatha," he whispers. "Are you all right?"

"I think so." I try to sit up, but my head goes all woozy.

"Move slowly," urges Jacoby.

The slam of a heavy metal door echoes in from the distance. I stiffen.

Jacoby leans down so we're nose-to-nose. "We don't have much time. They're coming."

My eyes widen. "Who?"

"My brother, King Gorgan. We're in his dungeons."

I blink hard, trying to process this information. *Total fail.* "But it was Froth and his buddies who attacked the cottage."

Jacoby's eyes glisten with sadness. "Not all my brothers are kind. Gorgan is obsessed that I'm a threat to him. He's been itching for an excuse to end my life for years. And if Mandrake told him that I might bond with you? That's plenty of reason for Gorgan to lock me up." He grasps the metal bars between our cells. "Whatever happens, you must pretend to still be passed out."

"I will."

Jacoby raises his hand. A dark sphere of power appears above his hand. The orb of power vanishes; Jacoby becomes a ghostly figure. At the same time, a duplicate version of Jacoby appears on the dungeon floor. The magical version of the prince seems to be solid and completely asleep.

Two people approach our dungeon cells.

One man wears a golden plague mask and fancy waistcoat. I'm guessing that's Kaiser Mandrake, the leader of the Minuscule. He's also the asshat who sent a plague army after me and Jacoby.

The second fellow must be Jacoby's brother, King Gorgan. That family is all about the power of large animals, and Gorgan wears the combination of a puffy shirt, leather vest, and animal-style war paint. *Subtle.* Gorgan also has horns, which must be a family trait. Only while Jacoby's are short, red, and curl forward, Gorgan's horns are white and remind me of a ram.

King Gorgan stares into the dungeons with a look combines self-pity, rage, and disgust... as if we're about to attack him for no reason at all.

The king seems determined to kill us first.

KING GORGAN

44

JACOBY

There are some things I've learned about my brothers. For instance, I know that I can create a double version of myself who seems to be asleep… and they'll never suspect that I'm actually awake and watching them carefully.

When it comes to Gorgan, I'm also confident of another fact: the man loves to hear himself talk. If my brother has the chance to impress Kaiser Mandrake, then he won't be able to resist. This is especially true if Gorgan thinks I'm passed out and won't hear a thing.

"You're certain they aren't really bonded?" asks Mandrake. Just like Froth, Mandrake's voice always sounds like many voices whispering at once. That said, the Kaiser always speaks with a particular edge of dull menace that's all his own.

"Not possible," answers Gorgan airily. "She doesn't have a secret elf name. I've sent animal spies to all the major elf settlements. They've no record of anyone like her. And without a tribe to raise you, you don't get a secret name. No name, no bonding, end of story."

This is a quirk of Mandrake, by the way. He's constantly asking questions that he already knows the answers to. It's his way of checking to see if you're trustworthy, full of real knowledge, or both.

For his part, Gorgan is oblivious to the fact that he was just put through a test. All he sees is a chance to look more informed and impressive to Mandrake.

"She's clearly a changeling," says Gorgan. "You know what that means."

A mixture of rage and fear churn through me. First, there's anger about the dismissive tone that my brother uses when talking about Agatha. Who cares if she's a changeling?

After that initial churn of rage, I'm swept up a second wave of chilly fear. What Gorgan and Mandrake don't know is the fact that Agatha does have a secret elf name. It's part of the spell put on her by her Moonbeam family. And if anyone knew this, Agatha and I wouldn't be imprisoned side by side. One or both of us would be dead.

Mandrake sighs. "It's a shame we have to turn her over to Nal'Adel."

Gorgan waves his hand dismissively. "Nothing to be done about it. The Queen of Moonshadow already has everything else she requires. Nal'Adel found the Vessel of Hours and the Eye of the World. All she needs is to take Agatha to the ruins and raise the Seelie imperials. Then the Queen of Moonshadow will become the most powerful fae ever."

Mandrake tilts his pointy head. "That doesn't worry you?"

"It would if we didn't have Agatha here. But we've been able to strike a good bargain in return for her. You and I won't suffer in Nal'Adel's new empire. What else is there to bother about?"

And this is why Gorgan is *not* my favorite brother. When the Essentials were handing out empathy powers, they passed right over our current king.

When Mandrake next speaks, his voice is extra low and biting. "Did you know any of the Seelie imperial family?"

"Why would I? I'm too young and besides, my house is aligned to the Unseelie."

"I knew them," says Mandrake.

Gorgan chuckles. "You know, you actually sound as if you regret that we won't meet these imperial losers."

"Perhaps I do."

"This is history, Mandrake. Both the Vessel and Eye are waiting right now in the Seelie ruins. Soon Nal'Adel will come here to claim Agatha. You have a front row seat to watch the birth of a new Empire. Nal'Adel won't let me anywhere near the place. You're lucky."

"I'm not going. I don't relish the idea of watching my old friends get consumed by Nal'Adel."

"She's just taking their magic."

"It's the same thing."

Gorgan's eyes widen. "I can't believe what I'm hearing. You really won't be joining Nal'Adel at the Seelie ruins?"

"No, I already have my unbreakable vows from you both. I kept my side of the bargain." Mandrake gestures toward Agatha as proof. "Now that I've delivered Agatha, you and Nal'Adel will be magically forced to hold to your word to my people as well. Nothing else matters."

A sly smile rounds Gorgan's mouth. "What was that promise again?"

My brother is such a bully. His favorite game when we were growing up was *hide the pet*. Whenever one of us would get attached to an animal, Gorgan would pretend our pet had disappeared. Now, he's playing the same game but with Mandrake. *Hide the agreement.*

But Mandrake isn't a child. He's a rather clever ruler and won't put up with Gorgan's games.

"Forget your vow and pay the consequences." Mandrake's body starts to dissolve. A haze of particles takes to the air. "No matter what happens, my people are independent. We will never be touched by Nal'Adel's new empire. Don't play around on this, Gorgan."

"Calm down, I was just kidding."

Mandrake's body reforms. "And *I'm* just being a good ruler to all my people."

Gorgan sniffs. "I take care of myself. That's what's best for everyone else."

This is another bit of classic wisdom from my brother. The man is such an ass.

"And what about your brother?" asks Mandrake. "How does his life serve yours?"

"If it were up to me, I'd have killed him already. But Nal'Adel wants him alive. She may need him as leverage to manipulate Agatha. That girl is the only one who can place the Eye into the Vessel." Gorgan stares at what he thinks is my sleeping form. For an instant, I think I catch a gleam of pity on his face. But it vanishes too quickly to be certain.

"Come along," announces Gorgan brightly. "I'll introduce you to my herd."

The two fae march away from the dungeons, leaving me and Agatha with a big question.

How do we stop Nal'Adel?

AGATHA

*O*nce Mandrake and Gorgan are gone, I reopen my eyes. This time, I feel healthy enough to sit upright. My fancy dress—or rather, Jacoby's long tunic—is now torn and covered in muck. It's the perfect symbol for my life right now. I pretend to be something I'm not and get ruined.

I should never have left New York. Not that I had much choice in the end. Eone and Skye were right. This quest would find me, no matter what. Not sure why magic chose me to restart the Seelie Empire, though.

Oh, well. Even magic makes mistakes.

Jacoby snaps his fingers. His fake double vanishes. There's no more illusion of the prince asleep on the floor. Instead, the real Jacoby stands above me. His hands grip the bars of the prison so tightly, his knuckles flare white.

"Did you hear that?" he asks.

"Every word."

"We must find a way to stop Nal'Adel when she shows up to claim you." Jacoby lets out a long breath. "Trouble is, I'm too tired to cast any major spells."

I nod. "And even if I were healthy, I have no idea how to wield my magic."

Jacoby crumples onto his knees, stopping when we're eye to eye. "Don't think that. We'll stop her somehow."

"Yes, we will."

Jacoby tilts his head. "What are you thinking?"

A dozen images fly through my mind at once. I picture Jacoby's herd—all those proud and intelligent animals who are now gone. I recall the tinge of worry in Eone's voice when the Essential talked about Elle. My stepsister is out there and at risk, same as Alec. Images from the Moonbeam Mirror flash through my head. In the reflection, I saw Seelie imperial running for their lives. How many of them could be brought back by the Vessel and the Eye?

I refocus on Jacoby. The sharp lines of his face are accented in the shadows of the dungeon. And his eyes hold so much longing and attachment, it's hard for me to hold his gaze.

Elle, Alec, the herd, the Seelie and Jacoby... I may have the power to save them all.

Harsh voices echo in the back of my head. *You're weak and a simpleton,* they say. *Don't bother—you're sure to fail.*

The speakers sound a lot like Marchesa and Ivy.

I may be everything you say, I reply in my mind. *But I can't turn away when I could try.*

So I take in a deep breath and reply to Jacoby's question.

"Here's what I think," I begin. "There's only one way out of this. Please, tell me your name. You already know mine. When we're fully bonded, we can share magic. I have plenty but I don't know how to use it."

Jacoby leans in so close to the bars, our faces are now only a few inches apart. His warm breath cascades over my mouth. "Are you sure?"

"Yes. Take my energy and get us out of here."

"Where would you want to go?"

"The Seelie ruins. Eone showed me what to do. I'll raise the Seelie and then they can help us end Nal'Adel. That's the real problem here. As long as I'm the only one who can hand over the keys to an Empire, I'll never be safe. We simply must become bonded."

A small grin rounds Jacoby's mouth. "And that's the only reason to become bonded? The need to stop Nal'Adel?"

This is it, Agatha. Might as well get this truth out.

"I heard what you said when I was poisoned... How you noticed me." I force myself to meet his gaze. Pure adoration shines out from the prince's eyes. "I love you too, Jacoby."

The prince nods. "My secret name is Hän Kesyttää Maailmaa. In English it means, *he tames the world.* Now you say it."

"Hän Kesyttää Maailmaa." The mark on my hip glows so brightly, it shines out through the fabric of my tunic. "And what's my name?"

"Hän Kävelee Kauneudessa. *She walks in beauty.*"

Suddenly, thin ribbons of blue magic materialize around us. Each line glows with power and light. The cords whip through the air and then loop round us, tying my hand to Jacoby's. Creating a line that extends between our hearts. And weaving into matching crowns that sit atop our heads.

A sense of warmth and affection moves through me. The sensation isn't coming from me. It's Jacoby's consciousness.

"Do you feel me?" he asks.

"I do."

"Normally, we'd have weeks to explore each other and find

out how we're connected. Every bonding is unique. But Nal'Adel could show up any second. I must access your magic."

"It's already yours."

A warm sensation swirls through me everywhere at once. Jacoby's love taps into the churn of power that's always been within my soul. Energy shifts along the ribbons between us, causing the lines to light up as my magic becomes his for a little while.

"That's enough," says Jacoby. "I must end the link."

This is the last thing I want, but I understand why it must be done. "Yes."

"Repeat after me," says Jacoby. "The bonding ceremony is over. Our names are shared."

I state the words Jacoby gave me. Light flashes on the cords between us. Then the ribbons disappear. Jacoby rises to stand. Lifting his arms, he summons a fresh sphere of power. The orb appears between his palms, then expands into a stone archway that spans our prison cells. On our side of the rocks, there's nothing but this nasty prison. But under the arch, I see a familiar space.

"That's the temple Eone showed me. Let's go!"

Jacoby and I lace our fingers together. Side by side, we step under the arch and into our only chance to stop Nal'Adel.

AGATHA

I step under the arch and into the temple. Up close, the place looks just like it did in my vision from Eone. Familiar patterns cover the walls and floor. Tall sconces cast pale light over the scene.

The place looks absolutely perfect. There are no chips in the stonework. No wiggly lines where someone messed up while painting a rune. It's almost too good to be real, but I suppose that's how things work when you're an Essential.

Still, I don't like it. Something here feels off.

Jacoby steps into the chamber. His mouth thins to a worried line. "I don't like this."

"Funny, I was thinking the same thing."

Jacoby raises his arms to chest height. Within seconds, a sphere of power appears between his palms. A mirror image of the temple interior appears inside the orb. "This place looks real enough, unless it's a layered illusion. But those are exceptionally rare."

A voice sounds from across the room. "Will you finish your quest or stand about?"

Looking over, I see Eone waiting at the far end of the chamber. She holds a large golden bowl in her arms.

My breath catches. "The Vessel of Hours. It's here."

"Yes," confirms Eone. "Now hold out your palm."

I'm still not sure about this whole thing, but I can't think of a good reason not to hold out my hand. Once I do, a flash of white light appears above my skin. When the brightness is gone, there's now a round crystal in its place.

The Eye of the World.

"Now come here," continues Eone. "Place the Eye of the World into this bowl. Help me bring back the missing Seelie imperial family."

I look to Jacoby. His face is pulled tight with anxiety. Worry twists inside me as well. Even so, I can't think of a good reason not to do what she says. This is what I want, right? Once I release the Seelie Imperials, then Nal'Adel has no reason to go after me.

What am I waiting for, anyway?

With hesitant steps, I cross the room and pause before Eone and the Vessel. The golden bowl is filled with water, just as I'd seen in my journey through time.

Raising my arm, I lift the Eye of the World so the stone is just a few inches above the water and bowl. Now, all I need to do is open my hand and drop the stone.

My hand twitches. Yet I don't release the Eye.

I snap my arm back. "No," I state. "This is wrong."

"Whatever do you mean?" asks Eone smoothly.

"This is too easy. That's not how my life works."

Eone's lovely face hardens with rage. "Put the Eye in the Vessel, Agatha."

Jacoby moves to stand at my side. "Watch yourself. Show the queen due respect."

Anger flashes across Eone's face. The glare stirs something inside me. Power churns in my soul. Connections align. Energy rises.

All of a sudden, I know exactly what's happening. I take a pointed step backward. Lowering my hand, I clutch the Eye tightly in my fist.

"This isn't happening," I state. "I know who you are, Nal'Adel."

Suddenly, the room transforms. Everything falls apart. The walls change into so many dying leaves. The Vessel vanishes. My hand—the one which clutches onto the Eye—becomes instantly empty.

A gust of wind blasts past me and Jacoby. The leaves burst apart, revealing that we don't actually stand inside a temple, Instead, we're at the very place where we waited after Jacoby took me to the Mirror of Moonbeams.

We're at the Seelie ruins.

Now Eone changes as well. The bits of her face and dress change into small dark leaves. These pieces of dying green peel away from Eone's body. When they're all gone, so is Eone.

Nal'Adel stands before us now.

And she holds a massive crossbow in her fist.

NAL'ADEL

JACOBY

*O**h, no.**

Now that the illusion is gone, it's clear that Agatha and I now stand atop the Seelie ruins. Nal'Adel waits nearby. The Vessel of Hours sits nearby. In Nal'Adel's right hand, she holds a metal crossbow. Her left hand clasps the Eye of the World.

It's a reflex to check my inner reserves of magic. The connection between me and Agatha stays strong. Emotion and energy flows between us. Thanks to our new bond, I can tap into this shared power. It's not an unlimited amount, but it should be enough for a fight, if it comes to that.

Who am I kidding? When it comes to a battle with Nal'Adel, it's not a question of *if*, it's *when*.

Nal'Adel rounds on Agatha. "What a shame. I made sure that Mandrake and Gorgan discussed all my plans in front of you both. I wanted you here. Don't you see? I was trying to make it easy for you."

"Thanks, but no thanks," snaps Agatha. Although she's

barefoot and standing in a torn tunic, I've never seen her appear more regal. "You've made a big mistake, Nal'Adel."

The elf queen smirks. "Have I?"

"Think." Agatha taps her temple. "I'm the only one who can place the Eye in the Vessel. You need me. Stop playing tricks."

My heart swells with pride. Like back at the cottage, Agatha is thinking quickly. I can see where she's going with this, so I step right in.

"Take a deep breath," I add. "Catch our scent."

Nal'Adel's nostrils flare as she inhales. I can see the moment when the realization hits her. Every muscle in Nal'Adel's body seems to tighten. "You're bonded."

"That's right," I state. "You can't fight us. How about we make a bargain instead? According to my brother, you're rather fond of those."

Nal'Adel narrows her eyes. "I'll consider it."

Agatha and I share a long look. My bonded offers me a shaky smile. I return the grin, although my expression is just as unsure. Sure, we can make a deal here. But some elves don't want bargains. They crave blood.

Meanwhile, Nal'Adel tilts her head, her eyes lost in thought. A spark of hope lights in my heart. Elves are notorious for their love of making deals.

Nal'Adel actually considering this. *Can we get out of this without anyone losing their life or soul?*

AGATHA

A *deal with Nal'Adel—this could work.*

My thoughts run through different ways to bargain with this evil queen. What am I willing to trade? I can't risk the people I care about. That said, there may be some way to magically ensure Nal'Adel gets a place in the Seelie Empire. She can't take in everyone's magic and soul... but maybe she'd be happy with a fancy title and some magical gemstones?

It's worth a conversation.

Nal'Adel smiles in that sweet way only the elves can manage. Then she moves with supernatural speed as she pulls up her crossbow.

Thwack!

Thwack!

Two bolts speed from the weapon at such velocity, I hardly register what's happening. Pain radiates from my upper arm. Looking down, I see a bolt sticking out from my skin. Jacoby hisses in a pained breath. Turning, I find that he's been hit with a bolt at the joint of his neck and shoulder.

Oh, no.

Even worse, black lines instantly radiate out from the spot on Jacoby's skin. Within seconds, the dark marks stretch down to the tips of his fingertips. I check my own hands. Black lines cover my flesh as well.

"Jacoby," I gasp.

He hisses in a pained breath. "This poison works fast."

No question what Jacoby means. When I was struck by the Shadow Morph's poison, it took many hours for the toxin to spread through my system. Jacoby and I won't last more than a matter of minutes.

My connection to Jacoby flares to life inside me. I can tell how much he's hurting. Casting spells is out of the question for both of us right now. One question rings through my mind.

Why?

I round on Nal'Adel. "What is this? You need me." Sadly, my voice is shaky. It's been less than a minute of poisoning, and I'm already having trouble pulling in enough breath. "I'm supposed to put the Eye in the Vessel."

A wicked smile curls Nal'Adel's mouth. "I sent that Shadow Morph after you as a test. I needed to see how you'd react to my poison. This particular venom is a new strain. It will force you to bend to my will before it kills you. So you see, I can simply command you to place the Eye in the Vessel. Believe me, you will do it."

Nal'Adel raises the bow once more. The weapon flares with white light before it transforms into a sword. She stalks toward me.

"Stay still," declares Nal'Adel. "Both of you."

Suddenly, I can't move. Jacoby doesn't shift, either. Through our bond, I can tell that he's as frozen as I am.

Nal'Adel issues her next command. "Raise your arm, Agatha."

With all my focus, I try to keep my hand down. Still, it's no use. My arm raises on its own.

A hungry gleam shines in Nal'Adel's eyes. "Call me old fashioned, but there are some things I like doing with my own two hands." She pauses before me and raises her sword high. "Or with your one hand, as the case may be."

Nal'Adel's plan comes into focus. My breath catches. The evil elf plans slice off my hand, place the Eye in my grasp, and then drop both into the Vessel.

"If you do this, I will cross all time and eternity to kill you," says Jacoby. His voice positively drips with menace.

"Silence, Jacoby." Nal'Adel keeps the sword at full height.

Then she starts to swing down.

Pink light flashes through the darkness. Cords of fairy dust slam into Nal'Adel's side, sending her toppling over. A figure steps into the place where the evil elf queen once stood.

It's Elle. And Alec is with her.

ELLE AND ALEC

49

ELLE

I turn over everything that's happened since Alec and I left the gemstone nursery.

Alec and I rush through darkened passages for what felt like hours. There are a lot of slippery rocks and tons of pokey stalag-thingys. One almost takes out my eye.

Finally, we reach the surface. We find a flat landscape that centers around a ruined temple. On the left side, there stretches a forest of bare trees. The opposite half of the scene is made up of low rubble and dead grass.

Squinting, I focus more closely on the temple itself. Three figures quickly become clear in the moonlight. I grasp Alec's forearm. "There they are," I state. "The one on the right is Nal'Adel. The other two are Agatha and Jacoby."

"See that?" asks Alec. He points toward something metal in Nal'Adel's hand. "It's a crossbow."

A fresh wave of worry moves through me. "Let's go."

There's no need for a long conversation between me and Alec. We both take off at a run. For my part, I've never missed my wings more. How much would I love to fly in this situation? Quite a lot.

Although my wings are gone, I do have access to my magic. As we closed in on the temple ruins, I summon up fresh cords of pink power and send them right at Nal'Adel. And I totally knocked that creep over. Go me.

Which brings me to the present moment.

I approach Agatha and Jacoby. My stepsister greets me with a smirk. "And here I was, planning to save you."

I wink. "You already did that once at the Glass Slipper Ball."

"I didn't realize you noticed," counters Agatha.

"It took me a little while," I say. "But I'm on it now." I turn to focus on Jacoby. His face is covered in a webwork of thin black lines. "You've looked better."

"It's poison," says Jacoby slyly. "Agatha has it, too. We'll figure something out."

I've known Jacoby all my life. There's a certain sneaky and overconfident air he gets when he's super-terrified. That's the exact kind of mojo that the guy is working now. I also know him well enough not to push him too hard when he's like this.

Jacoby may believe that he'll figure something out, but one this is for certain: he'll need some help.

Alec steps up. "Hey, there! I have no memory of the past, so don't assume I know anything. But I do answer to the name Alec."

Across the ruin, Nal'Adel rises. She glares at us and snaps her fingers.

I frown. That's it? *Snappy fingers. Oooooh, I'm sooooo frightened.*

All of a sudden, a whole army of Shadow Wraiths speed out of the nearby forest.

Okay, I take it back. That's what I call *pee-your-pants scary.*

WRAITH ARMY

50

ALEC

*N*ow, that's *a lot of Shadow Wraiths.*

Elle raises her hands. Lines of pink power weave around her fingertips. In this moment, she looks all things fierce and lovely.

Even so, frustration burns inside me. An army of disembodied torsos is heading our way, and I have no real options for fighting them.

Turning, I scan Agatha and Jacoby. The pair stand still as statues. With every passing second, the black lines of poison widen on their skin. It also seems to limit how much they can move. That won't end well.

Damn, I wish I had a gemstone. I rake my hands through my hair. *There must be something I can do.*

"Alec," whispers Jacoby. "Take my sword."

"Yes!." I pull the blade from Jacoby's hilt, get into battle stance, and prepare for onslaught.

As the wraiths close in, they stretch out their bony arms from under their cloaks. Each hand is tipped with razor-sharp fingers. They screech as they swoop in to attack. I swipe at them, but they are simply too many. It's all I can do to swat at them with my blade and try not to get skewered on their claws.

I glance over to Elle. She isn't doing much better. Long bolts of pink power erupts from her palms. The magical spears knock some Shadow Wraiths from the air. Others pin the creatures to the ground. Sadly, neither move holds the Wraiths down for long.

We're losing this fight.

In all the mayhem, I almost forget about Agatha and Jacoby. When I look over in their direction, it's already too late. Nal'Adel has somehow gotten both of them to stand before the Vessel of Hours. Agatha's arm is outstretched above the golden bowl.

The Eye of the World glistens in her fist.

Beyond the cries of battle, I can hear Nal'Adel issue her command to Agatha.

"Drop the Eye. Begin my reign."

Agatha moves to release the stone, but Jacoby somehow gains enough strength to reach out and clasp his own hands around Agatha's. Not sure how he manages it, either. The prince looks more dead than alive at this point.

Still, the Eye of the World stays in Agatha's grasp.

The world falls quiet. At first, I think it's a trick of the senses. I've heard such things can happen in battle. Then I realize that it's no illusion. The world is truly silent. Turning around, I discover the reason why.

A huge black dragon has landed on the ground behind me. And beyond the great beast, I can see hundreds of massive wolves waiting on the flatlands. These are no ordinary animals.

It's a shifter army.

Damn, I wish I had my memory back. Not that this isn't great, but I have a feeling I should be *really* enjoying whatever's happening now.

COLONEL MALLORY

51

ELLE

Please let this be real.
I blink.

Twice.

Three times.

Even so, the vision before me doesn't change.

Yes!

Colonel Mallory is here—and in his badass dragon form, no less. So are Bry, Knox, and their entire werewolf pack.

When I left my video message, I figured it would be nice to let them know what I'm up to. I didn't expect them to come charging after me.

Although, on second thought, I can't imagine them hanging around the apartment if they think I'm in danger, either.

Alec and I now stand on one side of the Seelie ruins. Jacoby, Agatha, and Nal'Adel wait in the center of the broken temple. Colonel Mallory looms across from me, on the other slope of the ruins. And behind him? There are wolves. Tons of them.

As for the Shadow Wraiths, they're now hovering in the air above me and Alec. None are attacking. My guess is that they realize they're right in spitting range of a fire-breathing dragon.

For floating torsos, they're pretty clever.

Dragon Colonel rakes his claws across the ground and glares at Nal'Adel. "I thought I made it perfectly clear to all of Faerie that Bryar Rose and Elle Cynder are under my protection. And here you are, sending Shadow Wraiths after Elle." He wags his head. "Bad form, Nal'Adel."

Nal'Adel blinks innocently. "Elle attacked me, Colonel. What was I supposed to do?"

Sure, I attacked Nal'Adel... after she locked up my boyfriend and tried to kill me with her Shadow Wraith. I happen to know that Colonel hates liars. This won't land well.

"It's more than that, though." As Dragon Colonel speaks, his mouth lights up from the angry fires burning within him. "You've been snooping around my personal business. Checking up on my little project at the pyramids. Using information that is not yours to send me off on a meaningless trip while you plot to take over Faerie."

Nal'Adel scowls. "Fidjit betrayed me. I'll kill him!"

"Nice thing about Fidjit," says Dragon Colonel. "He's always willing to sell information for a price. You really shouldn't have allowed him to leave your gemstone prison so easily. He could have gone anywhere. And he did."

Nal'Adel clasps the red stone that hangs at the base of her necklace. Odd to think I was trapped inside that thing. It's even stranger to realize that's actually part of her consciousness. The very thought makes me want to take a bath, pronto.

A long minute passes. The Shadow Wraiths hover. A werewolf howls. Dragon Colonel huffs out a long breath. Smoke curls up from his nostrils.

Nal'Adel rounds on Jacoby and Agatha. "Rise up!" she calls.

There are times in every caper where the world seems to move in slow motion. For instance, I'll never forget when I dropped an enchanted diamond ring into the Hudson. How long did it really take for that glittering thing to hit the water? One second, maybe two. In my mind, it was hours.

And that's exactly how I feel now. Whatever happens next is over with super quickly. It doesn't feel that way, though.

At Nal'Adel's command, a Shadow Morph oozes its way from under the rubble and wraps itself around Jacoby and Agatha. both become encased in darkness. The Shadow Morph forces Jacoby to tumble backward.

This is bad.

A moment ago, the prince had been clasping Agatha's hand and preventing her from dropping the Eye.

Now Jacoby is gone.

Meanwhile, Agatha remains entirely encased in the monster. Little by little, my stepsister's hand opens. Between the poison in her system and the Shadow Morph encasing her, Agatha doesn't stand a chance. She has to do what Nal'Adel commands.

The Eye of the World falls into the Vessel of Hours.

My stomach drops. Nal'Adel beams. As in, actual beams of blue light shoot off her arms and into the night sky as she shouts to the heavens.

"And now, my new empire begins!"

Dragon Colonel doesn't wait for more chatter. He lets loose a barrage of flames right at Nal'Adel's face. I wince, bracing for her to scream.

But she doesn't.

The fire engulfs Nal'Adel, but the blaze doesn't seem to hurt her at all. Talk about bad news.

The Shadow Wraiths now swoop into action. Dragon Colonel now focuses his fire on them. Turns out, they burn up pretty easily.

I pull on my own magic and send fresh ribbons of power over to Jacoby and Agatha. *Think you can wrap people up with magic? Two can play at that game.* I make my strips of energy surround both of my friends so the cords form a protective shield between their human bodies and the Shadow Morph.

Next I throw my arms backward. The motion makes my ribbons yank Jacoby and Agatha out of their gooey prisons. The pair fall onto the ground, free from any black goo. Agatha and Jacoby aren't free from their poison, but at least they aren't encased in a Shadow Morph any more.

That turns out to be a good news-bad news situation. On the plus side, Jacoby and Agatha are goop-less. Bringing up the negative, the original Morph now duplicates itself. In no time, a hundred Shadow Morphs now encircle the hilltop and Seelie ruins.

The werewolves go to work. They hunt in packs, driving the Shadow Morphs into the line of Dragon Colonel's fire.

In short order, both the Morphs and Wraiths are gone. *Yay, teamwork!* Dragon Colonel refocuses on Nal'Adel. "Let's try this again," he growls. "Pay attention when I'm talking to you."

All this time, Nal'Adel has been reaching up to the sky. Now she lowers her arms. A great figure descends from the clouds. It seems to be made from the very kind of gemstones that Alec and I saw in the nursery.

"If you wish to bargain," says Nal'Adel. "You'll have to get past my Goliathae."

I shift my gaze to Dragon Colonel. For all I know, a Goliathae is a total battle wimp. Dragon Colonel sizes up the massive creature. Then I see it. A flicker of worry shines in his serpentine eyes.

Oh, we are so screwed.

52

ALEC

The largest supernatural gemstone on record is about the size of my fist. Now, there's a six-story-tall woman warrior floating above me who's made up of nothing but magic crystal.

I can't even imagine what she's capable of.

Strike that. I've got a few concepts. None of them are good.

The Goliathae moves as fast as lightning. First, she turns on Dragon Colonel. The Goliathae lifts her arms with her palms flat. Long crystals whip out from her palms. The blade-like stones puncture the Colonel's dragon hide. Blood oozes from the wounds. More crystals tear through his wings.

Dragon Colonel hobbles forward. The Goliathae sends a fresh volley of crystals into his body. These are long as blades and bite deeply into his flesh. Dragon Colonel crumples onto his side, dead.

I must know this Colonel in my real life, because I stifle the urge to wail.

Goliathae now focuses on the werewolves. Fresh waves of

crystals shoot out from her hands, taking down a hundred wolves at once.

Next she turns on me.

Goliathae sends twenty crystal blades in my direction. I try to dodge, but there are too many. A sad thought hits me.

I'm about to die, and I don't even know who I am.

At the last moment, a huge black wolf leaps into the air between me and the Goliathae. The shifter takes all the crystal daggers at once. He falls to the ground and transforms into a man with ice-blue eyes and heavy black hair.

I rush to his side. "Why did you do that?"

"You'd do the same for me," he says.

Elle mentioned this guy before. I don't remember him at all, but if these are Knox's last moments, then I'm not going to ruin them with a discussion of my magical amnesia.

"Yeah, Knox. I would."

The man reaches into his pocket and pulls out a large pink diamond. "It's the color of Elle's magic. Thought you might like it."

I take the stone and turn it over in my palms. It's been so long since I held a powerful gem. Now I feel as if part of my soul has been restored.

"Thank you," I say quietly.

"Now take down that sparkly menace," says Knox. A line of blood trickles from his mouth.

"No, I can use this to heal you." I grip the stone in my right hand while I touch Knox's shoulder with my left.

It's no use.

He's already dead.

White-hot rage pumps through my bloodstream. Rising, I

grip the stone with both hands, holding it high above my head.

And I focus my spell on Goliathae.

All my pain and regret combines with the magic of the stone. A beam of pale red light shoots into the sky and lands right onto Goliathae's heart.

Crack!

A spiderweb of breaks appears on her torso. I press the magic further, using the stone to tap into the inner energy I carry with me always.

The lines of breakage spread. Goliathae hunches over. I double the power and strength of my spell.

Thwack! Thwack! Thwack!

Something strikes me in the back. My body turns numb. Looking over my shoulder, I find three silver bolts in my spine. And beyond that? I see Nal'Adel.

Her crossbow stays aimed in my direction.

53

ELLE

The battle rages all around me. I can't seem to care. It took me a while, but I found the body of a white wolf.

Dead.

It's Bryar Rose. Her rib cage is torn up from all the crystal daggers. Tears cloud my vision and my voice chokes.

"Why did you have to come after me?" I kneel beside her body and pick the crystal blades from her chest. My hands become covered in blood.

At some point, I'm vaguely aware that Goliathae is in trouble. Her body is cracking. She's actually hunching over instead of shooting out more daggers.

I scan the ruins. Then I see him.

Alec.

Pink light is shining out from a gemstone in his hands. My breath catches. Maybe I can't save Bryar Rose, but I certainly can avenge her. I race across the battlefield.

I'm only a few yards from Alec when it happens.

Three silver bolts strike his back. Alec falls over. I rush to his side. This can't be happening again. *Didn't I just leave Bryar Rose?*

I kneel down for a better look. Alec lies curled on his side. His skin is already covered in what looks like thick black lines. Poison. I take his hands in mine.

"Hang on, Alec. I'll figure out some way to fix this."

He gives my hands a gentle squeeze. "My memory still isn't back, but I'm not sure that matters. Whoever I am, I can't stop falling for you." He closes his eyes. I check his pulse.

He's gone, too.

Goliathae hovers above me. The cracks in her body are starting to heal. It won't be long before she starts fighting again.

I'm the last one alive on the battlefield.

Something weighs down the pocket of my sweater. Reaching inside, I find a yellow bottle with a silver stopper.

Memories flicker through my mind. This is how it happened to Skye. She found her bottle and became a genie. Now, at last, her story makes sense. Everyone I love is gone. It's time to become someone different.

And if being a genie means I can destroy Nal'Adel and the Goliathae? Count me in.

I uncork the small bottle. Tendrils of mist slink out from the container. They quickly expand until I'm surrounded in a small cloud of power. I start to change. Before, I wore jeans and a sweater. Now, I'm in a formal dress. I pat my head. Even my hair is done up.

This is me, part way to becoming a genie.

Remembering my trip through time, I speak the words that will complete my transformation and seal my fate.

"I am Elle Morningstar."

ELLE

54

ELLE

My body erupts into mist. I become everything and the void, all at once. My consciousness swirls down to take up residence in the bottle, yet I'm also outside the container, watching it all happen.

My cloudy self spirals out of the bottle. I retake my human form. Knowledge spins through me and becomes me. Every fact about what I am and how I work becomes clear as a morning star. No wonder we all take the name.

I am a genie. And I know how to kick some ass.

"I wish this Goliathae chick would blow the hell up."

The massive creature vibrates. Red light spreads through her crystalline body. For a moment, all is silent.

Then she explodes.

Tiny bits of stone fall all around, tinkling as they hit the ground and each other.

I stalk up to the center of the Seelie ruins. Nal'Adel stands there, waiting for me.

"So, you think you're a genie."

I make my legs do that smoke-move I've seen on Skye a dozen times. "I am a genie."

Nal'Adel frowns. "I'm stronger than Eone, Skye, and you... and I haven't yet consumed any magic from any of the Seelie imperial family. Just watch what I do next. Your petty powers won't be able to stop it. I shall—"

Nal'Adel stops speaking. Looking down, she sees that the tip of a sword blade had now popped through her chest. Agatha steps around. She's not looking healthy, but the girl has somehow found the strength to grab Nal'Adel's old sword and wield it. Something in my new genie senses tells me this has something to do with her new bond to Jacoby. That's a lot of information, so I set it aside for later.

"How can this be happening?" asks Nal'Adel. "You're worthless." The elf queen crumples to her knees.

Agatha stalks over so she's eye-to-eye with Nal'Adel. "All my life, I've wasted time letting other people tell me what I am. But now, in this moment, I see the truth. I am Queen Kir'Atha, Agatha, and a bonded elf. You've hunted me down and harmed those I love."

"I still..." Nal'Adel pulls in a rasping breath "...don't understand."

Agatha rises to her full height. "I'm the chosen one, bitch."

Nal'Adel falls over, dead.

ELLE

I want to do a happy dance about Agatha finally taking down Nal'Adel, but there isn't time.

There's a lot of wishing to do.

I speak my desires in rapid fire. I ask for my friends to come back to life... Nal'Adel to stay dead forever... the Seelie imperial family to return... and for Alec to remember me. I'm running out of good ideas when it happens.

The ground rumbles. The skies clear. A golden city lowers from the heavens.

My genie sense knows what this is.

The Seelie Imperial Palace is coming back.

SEELIE RETURNS

56

AGATHA

*D*aylight streams all around me as the great Seelie Imperial Palace lowers from the sky to land on the hilltop. I can't help but notice how the new structure flattens the old ruins while burying what's left of Nal'Adel.

Somehow, that's really fitting.

A nearby ground rumbles, then breaks as a single blue crystal juts up from the earth.

The azure gemstone shimmies and then vanishes. An elf woman in a green dress steps forward.

"I am Lady Bluebell of the Flora," she announces. "I have been brought back by Eone." The way she speaks these words, it's as if she were dropping off her dry cleaning. Maybe it's a side effect of being raised an elf, but these folks are experts at hiding any extreme emotions.

Except Jacoby. But he's awesome that way.

Across the scene, more crystals rise up from the ground. More elves are released. They announce themselves and start to set up a party in their new Imperial Palace. Some take up musical instruments. Others conjure food.

I turn around, ready to find Jacoby, Elle, and maybe something to eat.

Sadly, I don't get too far.

Marchesa and Ivy block my path.

"You've ruined everything," says Marchesa. "Again."

"We had an alliance with Nal'Adel," whines Ivy. "Now what are we going to do?"

The ground rumbles beneath my feet yet again. This round is the most forceful yet. I frown. "I think some more crystals might be rising. We should get out of the way."

Marchesa rolls her eyes. "The crystals are appearing over in the Seelie place, you stupid girl. I think—"

In that moment, a bunch of things happen at once. Jacoby grabs me from behind and pulls me away from Marchesa and Ivy. A massive herd of magical animals stampedes right over the spot where I was just standing.

Jacoby flips me around so we're facing one another. "Guess what?" he says with a sneaky grin. "It seems my herd has been released from prison." He goes on tiptoe to scan over my shoulder. "And Marchesa and Ivy didn't act quickly enough to get out of the way. Pity."

I wince. "Is there anything to… take care of?"

"The short answer is *no*. You'll never see Marchesa and Ivy again. It's really best if we leave it at that."

"Fine. I'll categorize it under *supernatural side effects of a magical herd*."

"Good idea."

A pulse of power moves across our bond. I tighten my grip on Jacoby's shoulders. "What's happening?"

"Can't you feel it through our connection? You're taking your final true form." Jacoby summons an orb of power and opens a portal. I can feel his excitement through our link. "Shall we?" asks Jacoby.

"Whatever you're up to, I'm in."

Jacoby scoops me in his arms and walks under the stone archway that's his favorite type of portal. We march out onto the top of a silver palace that's topped by conical towers. Moonbeams reflect off the metallic surface and into the green forests beyond.

"This is yours," says Jacoby. "It's the Moonbeam palace. I believe it's only proper for a Moonbeam queen to take her final form while surrounded by beauty."

Light emanates from my pores. I feel my ears lengthen farther. My hair turns an even more vivid shade of red. My ripped tunic transforms into elven jewels and silk.

I become who I was always meant to be.

AGATHA

JACOBY

I set my bonded back onto her feet. "You're beyond lovely, Agatha."

She blushes ever so slightly. "Thank you, Jacoby. For everything."

My heart soars as a realization overtakes me. I cup Agatha's face in my hands. "All my life, I've only sought to protect myself from pain. But you changed my future, Agatha. Now my days will focus on giving you joy. You can't imagine what a wonderful gift that is for someone like me."

And I guide our lips together for a kiss.

AGATHA

*J*acoby's lips gently brush against mine. Our kiss quickly turns fierce. I link my arms around his neck and enjoy every sensation—both his and my own—as they flow through me.

It's Jacoby who breaks the kiss. "Now that you've seen your palace, where do you want to be?"

I know what he means here, and I have the perfect reply ready.

"Well," I begin. "Someone needs to get the herd back to the fields, right?"

Through our bond, I sense the jolt of Jacoby's happiness at my reply.

"Yes," says the prince. "They do."

"In that case, let's go home."

"Are you sure? What about Cynder Mercantile?"

"Just hanging around there gave me nightmares. I was stuck on it because I didn't give myself any other choices. But now? I see nothing but possibilities for us."

We share another smile and a gentle kiss before stepping off into Jacoby's latest portal, hand in hand.

ELLE

*O*ne thing the Seelie know, and that's how to throw a party. Soon, everyone is celebrating. Hundreds of Seelie imperials are singing, gabbing or eating. Bry, Knox, and the Colonel are owning the dance floor. Agatha and Jacoby took off, but they looked pretty blissed out then they did it. I don't think we'll see them again soon.

Not that I'm jealous.

Okay, maybe I'm toting around a little bit of envy.

I search out the crowd for Alec. He stands aloof. I wave in his direction. I can't help but shoot him a hopeful smile. After all, I made a wish that he'd get his memories back. The question is there, if unspoken.

Do you remember me now?

Alec shakes his head. My heart cracks. The meaning is clear.

No, I don't remember you.

"And now I'm a genie," I mutter. "Which means I'll spend an eternity alone. I just wish I had Alec back."

A small tornado of smoke appears beside me. When the storm ends, marshal Skye stands in its place. "Hey, sister."

I shrug. "Hi."

"I know you made that wish about Alec," continues Skye. "But it doesn't work that way. We genies stay solo. Any chances for romance just don't work with our magic."

Another shrug. "Oh."

Skye lets out a long groan. "Fine. Just this once, maybe I can grant a few wishes for you."

My body turns numb with shock. "You don't mean…"

Another cloud appears. This time, it's Eone who shows up. She wags her finger at Skye. "This is why you don't have many genies. You keep going soft and letting them off the hook."

"Yeah, but can you blame me?" asks Skye. "She just saved all our asses."

"No, I guess I can't blame you. This time."

Skye taps her chin. "While I'm at it, I'll make a few other improvements on your life. You're welcome."

Suddenly, this is seeming like it might be a crap idea. "Skye making life improvements could be a disaster. "What do you plan to do?"

Fresh plumes of magic smoke surround me. Energy and power skitter across my skin. The glass jar shatters in my hand.

I'm no longer a genie.

Skye's wish isn't over yet. My long gown changes to a short white dress. A thin crown of leaves encircles my head. And light erupts across my shoulder blades.

I have wings.

Joy balloons through my soul as I take to the air.

ALEC

*L*eaning back on my heels, I watch Elle unfurl her wings and take to the sky. I've never seen anything more beautiful.

And Elle is always saying that she feels her wings sometimes. She must feel beyond happy to have them back.

My skin prickles over into gooseflesh. *Hold on, there.* Did I just have a memory?

I think I did.

Elle swoops down to gracefully land before me. She looks so forlorn and alone. I take her hands in mine.

"I remember you."

Elle narrows her eyes. "Really?"

"I remember how you always call puppies your boo babies. The way you elbow strangers to get a better place on the subway. How you make every day something to smile about." I run my palms up her arms. "I remember you, Elle...

...I love you."

ELLE

*M*y soul overflows with joy. *We're back. Truly.*

I smile from ear to ear. "I love you, too Alec."

A sky look comes over his handsome face. "I saw you talking with Skye. What are you these days? A genie?"

"I'm a Cinderella and a genie and a warden. I'm the girl who loves Alec Le Charme and cherishes my friends. Most of all, I'm just Elle. And that's whatever I want it to be."

Alec gives me another of his perfect, million-watt smiles. "And I've always loved that about you."

We share a kiss, and for the first time in ages, my life feels right, true and eternal.

—The End—

The Unseelie fae get rowdy in Fairies and Frosting, Book 7 of the Fairy tales of the Magicorum

FAIRIES AND FROSTING - DESCRIPTION

The adventure continues with FAIRIES AND FROSTING Fairy Tales of the Magicorum #7!

~

About FAIRIES AND FROSTING

At last, Elle (never call her Cinderella) is reunited with Alec, the Prince of Le Charme Jewelers. *Yay!* But the pair soon discovers that Alec's gemstone empire is about to go bankrupt. *Boo.* So our favorite couple devises a kick-ass scheme to save Le Charme. To announce their plan, Elle and Alec will hold a Glass Slipper Festival complete with music, dancing and cake. Lots of cake.

There's only one problem. ***The Unseelie fae have returned.***

Talk about bad news. No one combines lovely looks with dark intentions better than the Unseelie. Now, those nefarious fae want to destroy Elle, Alec and any hope for Le Charme. It doesn't end there, either. The Unseelie are also targeting Elle's stepsister, Agatha, as well as her old friend, Jacoby. And when will the Unseelie launch their deadly schemes? The Glass Slipper Festival.

Because fairies and frosting don't mix.

Fairy Tales of the Magicorum

Modern fairy tales with sass, action, and romance

1. Wolves and Roses
2. Moonlight and Midtown
3. Shifters and Glyphs
4. Slippers and Thieves
5. Bandits and Ball Gowns
6. Fire and Cinder
7. Fairies and Frosting
8. Towers and Tithes
9. Evil Queens and Goblin Kings

ALSO BY CHRISTINA BAUER

FAIRIES AND FROSTING

BOOK 6, FAIRY TALES OF THE MAGICORUM

Elle, Alec and their friends return in FAIRIES AND FROSTING!

ANGELBOUND

Check out ANGELBOUND, the kick-ass paranormal romance! Read on for a sample…

PIXIELAND DIARIES

PIXIELAND DIARIES tells the story of sassy pixie Calla and 'her' elf prince, Dare.

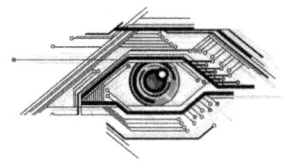

A kick-ass heroine + a swoon-worthy prince + an all-girl heist
= SCYTHE!!!

BEHOLDER

Medieval mages … Slow-burn love … And heart-pounding action! Check out the BEHOLDER series!

*I*t's been one month, three days, and six hours since I last 'got my gladiator on' and battled in the Arena. Not that I'm obsessing or anything. Sure, I can sneak in and watch someone else fight, but that's a snore.

I roll over on my dingy bed, scooch under the drab covers, and watch the gray drizzle outside my window. Mondays are the pits.

Mom's voice echoes into my bedroom. "Time to get up! You don't want to be late for school, do you, honey?"

I roll my eyes. *Of course,* I want to be late for school.

Raising my head, I open my mouth to say just that, and then decide against it. Instead, I bite my lower lip, yank the pillow over my head and groan. Loudly.

"Don't make noises at me, young lady." Mom rustles papers in the kitchen. "I've a letter right here. You're on something called the Official Watch List for Unreasonable Tardiness." Her footsteps echo down the hall and pause outside my room. "You'll be suspended from high school at this rate. What do you think about *that?*"

I peep out from under my pillow. Mom looms in my doorway, her fist set on her hip. She's a quasi-demon like me, so she resembles a lovely human with a curvy figure, amber skin, chocolate-brown eyes, and chestnut hair that falls in waves over her shoulders. All quasis have a tail; Mom and I both sport the long and pointed variety. The big differences between us are laugh lines, some grey hair and our opinion of what's 'dangerous' for eighteen-year olds.

I fluff the pillow and slide it under my noggin. Being suspended means no school. Maybe even catching a few Arena matches on the sly. I wag my eyebrows. "And suspension would be bad because?"

"I'd make it that way."

Ugh. She would, too.

Off go my covers. "This is me getting up."

"Good." Mom stomps away.

I shower, pull on some sweats, and sleepwalk into the kitchen, seeing the familiar lime-green appliances, mismatched furniture, and peeling linoleum tile. Everything looks peaceful, quiet, and empty. Another typical Monday morning before another average day at school. *BO-ring.* I'll have to charm Walker into taking me to the Arena later. Until I'm called to fight again, it's better than nothing.

A thick white envelope sits at the center of the kitchen table. I scoop up and read: "To the Quasi-Demon, Miss Myla Lewis, 666 Dante Row, Purgatory." I lick my thumb and run it over the loopy calligraphy. *Real ink.* My long black tail flicks in a nervous rhythm.

Frowning, I tap the unopened letter against my palm. No one sends me fancy stuff like this. In a blur of motion, my tail darts across my torso, grips the envelope with its arrowhead-shaped end, and tries pulling it from my fingers.

"Hey now!" My tail's always had a mind of its own. For some reason, it's decided this letter is dangerous. I jerk the envelope out of reach, but not before one corner gets totally shredded. "Now, look what you did." My tail slinks behind me to curl guiltily about my ankle.

I reread the outside of the letter. Nothing here to worry about. I *am* a quasi-demon (mostly human with a little demon DNA). I've spent all eighteen years of my life in Purgatory (where human souls get judged for Heaven or Hell, aka the most boring place in the history of ever). This letter's like dozens of others that hit our doorstep each week. Why's my tail on a mission to trash this thing?

I stare at the words again, feeling like they should read: "Open this to turn your life upside-down and your heart into mush."

Clearly, I'm having an off-morning.

I slip the envelope-slash-time-bomb into my mangy back-pack. I'll read it later at school.

Mom steps into the kitchen. "How's my sweet baby, Myla-la?" Yes, I'm eighteen years old and Mom still uses pet names from when I was three.

"I'm good." I open a cabinet and pull down a box of Frankenberry cereal.

Mom eyes my every movement, her forehead creasing with worry.

"Did you sleep well last night, Myla?"

Oh, no. Here it comes. I square my shoulders and mentally prepare my 'I'm so very-very caaaaaaalm' voice. "Absolutely." *Nailed it.*

"Any bad dreams?"

"Nope." The 'calm voice' isn't working so well this time.

"Hmm." She taps her cheek. "Met anyone lately? Made any new friends?"

I grit my teeth. All my mornings start off with maternal interrogations like this one. I find it's best to give soothing, one-word answers. "Negative."

"No friends at all?"

"Only the same one since first grade." I raise my spoon for emphasis. "Cissy."

"That's good." She offers me a shaky grin. "You're safe."

I shoot her a hearty thumbs-up. Today's cross-examination ended relatively quickly; maybe Mom's getting less overprotective. A grin tugs at the corner of my mouth.

"More than safe." I speed-chop the air, karate-style. "I'm a lean, mean, Arena-fighting machine." Wincing, I freeze midchop. *How could I be so dumb?* Mom loses her freaking mind whenever I say the word 'Arena.'

There's a pause that lasts a million years while Mom stares at me, her face unreadable. Finally, she moves. But, instead of jumping around in hysterics, she flips about and rifles through cabinets in search of a coffee mug.

Wait a second.

This morning Mom cut her interrogation short *and* she didn't panic when I said the word 'Arena.' I wind my lips into an even-wider grin. Sweeeet. Things *could* be changing, after all.

Leaning back in my chair, I watch Mom pour coffee. I know she goes overboard because it's just me, her, and this nasty gray ranch house. I have no brothers, sisters, or straight answers about who my father is, except that he's some kind of diplomat. Add it all up and Mom's a wee bit clingy.

Or, at least, she *used* to be. I drum my fingers on the Formica. A less overprotective Mom opens up all sorts of possibilities. I could watch more matches. I could fight in more matches. I could develop interests in things other than the Arena.

Eh, maybe it's a 'no' on that last thing.

Mom slides into the chair across from mine, her large brown eyes watching me through the wisps of steam curling from her mug. "Want a ride to school today? I don't mind waiting outside the door." A muscle twitches at the corner of her eye. "You know, in case anything happens."

My heart sinks to my toes. Then again, maybe Mom's worse than ever.

"Uhhhh." My mouth falls so far open, some Frankenberry rolls off my tongue and onto the tabletop. Did she *really* offer to stand outside school all day long 'in case anything happens?' Cissy told me how parents get extra-twitchy during senior year. A shiver rattles my spine. My Mom *plus* 'extra-twitchy' *equals* a huge nightmare.

I force a few deep breaths. "Thanks for the offer." It's getting really hard to keep my 'calm voice' handy. "I'll pass this time."

Suddenly, the air crackles with energy. A black hole seven feet high and four feet wide appears in the center of the kitchen.

Out of the void steps a ghoul.

My fingers twiddle in his direction. "Hey, Walker." Technically, he's named WKR-7, but I've called him Walker for as long as I can remember.

"Good morning." Walker nods his skull-like head. If he were a few inches taller, the movement would knock his cranium through ceiling, and he's on the short side for a ghoul. It's a mystery how Walker and the rest of the undead-lies handle an eternity of being so crazy-tall.

Walker pulls back his low-hanging hood, showing pale, almost colorless skin and a strong bone structure. He sports the same hairstyle from the day he died: a brush cut with side-burns and no beard. Great black eyes peep at me from deep sockets.

I grin. It's nice to have Walker around. Most ghouls are obsessed with rules and act irritating as Hell. But Walker? He pushes boundaries like a pro, especially when it comes to sneaking me into the Arena. Having him around is like having a cute and somewhat sneaky older brother, only one without a pulse.

"Be careful, Myla." Walker's thin lips droop into a frown. "That's no way to greet your overlords. I don't mind, but other ghouls could send you to a re-education camp."

I roll my eyes. Purgatory is one massive bureaucracy with the charm of suburbia and the fun of a minimum-security prison. All the work's done by unpaid quasis like me (we're not allowed to call ourselves 'prisoners'). Ghouls keep us in line and make sure we're–*cough, cough*–super happy in our service.

I'm ready to complain about all this to Walker for the millionth time when Mom pipes into the conversation.

"Greetings, my beloved overlord." She's laying it on thick to make up for my sloppy hello. "Want some decaf?" She bows.

Walker nods; ghouls love java.

Mom picks up one of Walker's loopy sleeves, rubbing the fabric between her fingertips. "This is a little threadbare. Are you here for a new one?" All quasis must perform a service; Mom sews and mends robes. It could be worse. My friend Cissy's mom is a ghoul proctologist.

"No, thank you." Walker eyes the coffee pot greedily.

Mom hands him a full mug marked 'Afterlife's Greatest Ghoul.' Her chocolate eyes nervously scan his face. "What service do you require then?"

Walker frowns. "Myla must battle in the Arena today."

A huge grin spreads across my face. When human souls reach Purgatory, they're given a choice: trial by jury, or trial by combat. Based on the result, they end up either happily floating around Heaven or having their souls consumed in Hell. If the human selects a trial by jury, then it's someone else's problem. But if they choose combat–and the combatant in question is totally evil–then someone like Walker ends up in the kitchen of someone like me. I'm one of a few dozen quasis who kick butt. Literally.

I jump to my feet and clear off my bowl. "Now, this is what I call a Happy Monday."

Mom steps back. "You're sending Myla off to fight today? You can't." She leans against the countertop for support. "Every time she goes, she risks her life." A muscle twitches by her mouth. "Those battles are *to the death*."

I stifle a moan. Mom always focuses on the whole 'to the death' thing like it's the first time she's learned how matches work. Hell, I've battled in the Arena since I was twelve and have yet to get a scratch. You'd think the drama would tone down over the years.

Panting, Mom points to a tattered calendar by the door.

"My little one fought a month ago. She serves once every *three* months, right?"

I raise my hand. "It's not a problem. I'm up for this. Totally."

Mom flashes me a desperate look. "I know that." She grips the countertop like she'll pull it out of the wall. "Please, Walker, tell me it's a mistake."

Walker's black eyes fill with understanding. "Myla must serve today. There's a spike in Arena matches; all fighters have extra battles."

Mom stares at Walker, her jaw grinding out silent rebuttals. After a few moments, she presses her palms to her face, a low sigh escaping her lips. I frown. She's hitting a new level of drama this morning.

Walker shoots me the barest wink. I fight the urge to smile, knowing it means one thing: there's no across-the-boards spike in Arena matches. Purgatory must have an uber-evil soul on their hands, the worst of the absolute worst, and they need their best fighter on it.

That would be me.

Mom shakes her head from side to side. "All those demons and angels. Promise me, you'll keep her away from 'danger.'" She puts special emphasis on the word 'danger.'

"I always do, Camilla."

Mom releases her death-grip from the counter. "Of course."

My back teeth lock. Mom's always going on about protecting me from angels and demons. The demons I understand, but *angels*? Come on.

I zip up my gray hoodie. "Time to trash some evildoers." Stepping to Walker's side, I wait for transport to the Arena.

Mom's hand lightly touches her throat. "Be safe!"

"I'll be super-safe, don't you worry."

"And don't be late for school."

I slap on a smile. "On it, Mom."

Walker bows his head. "Stand back, I'll summon a portal." A new black hole appears in the center of the kitchen. I glance into the darkness, feeling the Frankenberry in my belly come up for a repeat performance. Using a portal feels like tumbling through empty space with a killer case of the stomach flu. Helpful safety tip: hold a ghoul's hand or you'll fall forever.

Taking a deep breath, I grab Walker's chilly fingers so tightly, I'd cut off his blood flow, if he had any. Together, we step into the portal, topple through nothingness, and walk out again onto the sandy earth of the Arena floor. I try my best to look ready-for-battle instead of ready-to-puke.

Walker offers me a sympathetic glance. "Shall we find a place to sit?"

"Nah, I'm fine, thanks." I scan the open-air stadium around me. The Arena's a nasty old ruin, all chipped gray rock and busted sandstone columns. How the place stays upright is a total mystery. The fighting floor is one huge uneven clod of dirt, the bleachers are basically rubble, and the entire top level looks ready to collapse.

I freaking love it here.

The stands lie open and empty, except for a few quasis. They're all fighters like me, trying to catch someone else's match. Mom used to attend too, but all the moaning and gasping got so out of hand, she was banned ages ago. I can't say I was bummed. Nothing like having your Mom yell 'Baby, don't diiiiiiiiiiiiiiiiie' when you're twelve and fighting a demon for the first time.

A gravelly voice echoes through the air. "Greetings, *slave*." The word 'slave' is said with particular venom.

Every muscle in my body goes on alert. I'd know that voice anywhere, and I absolutely loathe its owner. I scrape lint from under my fingernails and pretend not to notice the seven-foot tall ghoul looming behind me.

Walker steps between us. "Greetings, SKE-12."

My mouth winds into a mischievous grin. "Hey, Sharkie.'" SKE-12 hates his nickname, so I work it into every encounter.

Sharkie frowns. "My name is SKE-12, *slave*."

Walker sets his hand on my shoulder, gently guiding me so I stand face-to-navel with Sharkie, master of Arena ceremonies and all-around dickhead. He hasn't changed a bit since my last match, not that ghouls often do. He's gray-skinned with large coal-black eyes, a skull-like hole for a nose, and teeth that have been filed to tiny points. His long silver robes hang in tatters; a tall black staff is gripped in his bony hand.

Walker gives my shoulder a squeeze. "Myla was just about to greet her ghoul overlord properly, weren't you, Myla?" Standing next to Sharkie, even Walker looks vertically challenged.

"My bad." I bow extra-low. "Greetings, SKE-12."

His buggy black eyes narrow into slits. Sharkie always knows when I'm making fun of him, and it drives him crazy. "I'll have no mischief from you today."

I bow again, even lower this time. "Yes, I'm fresh out."

Sharkie turns to Walker, his black eyes flaring bright red. "Control her." His gaze swings back to me. "We've an especially evil human soul fighting today. I hope to watch you die at last."

I pick something off my molar with my pinky. "I'm sure you do."

Sharkie steps closer, his pointy teeth click-clacking as he speaks. "The soul you fight today is so evil, the angels have begged the Great Scala to stand by, ready to transport him to Hell the moment he's defeated. Which will never happen." He leans in closer. "You. Are. Doomed."

My brows pop up. Normally, the Scala migrates tons of souls at once in what's called an iconigration. For this guy to get solo treatment, he must be a SUPER nasty. *Fun.* "Bring it on, Shar−."

Walker grabs my elbow. "Look, Myla! Your friends are here!" He points across the stadium floor. "We must depart." He bows once more to Sharkie. "Excuse us." As we speed-walk away, Walker whispers in my ear. "If I weren't already dead, I'd have had a heart attack just now."

"Eh, Sharkie's harmless."

"Because I placate him for you." He shoots me a sly look. "Why must you always taunt him?"

"Not sure." I shrug. "It's a hobby." A few yards ahead stands a ghoul named XP-22, and a hovering green blob that's Sheila, the Limus demon.

I shoot Sheila a friendly wave. "Hey Shiel, how are the kids?" Sheila's nice, so long as you don't stand close enough for her to swallow you whole. XP-22, on the other hand, is a total drip. I don't even glance in his direction.

"The kids are good, Myla, getting bigger every day...Just like you." Sheila's entire body shivers, which is a little scary since she's six feet tall, three feet wide, and has fourteen red eyes the size of tennis balls. "It seems like yesterday you were twelve and about to fight your first demon." Her huge gaping mouth twists into a grin. "How old are you now, honey?"

"Eighteen."

A blob-like arm stretches out from Sheila's side, lengthening into a gooey hand with eighteen long fingers. "Almost grown up! Have you been assigned your service yet?" 'Assigning your service' is ghoul-speak for locking a quasi into a life-long job after high school. We're not allowed to call it 'prison labor.' I shiver. There are some mighty foul careers out there too, like the infamous anal probe development lab.

Before I can reply to Sheila's question, Sharkie thumps his staff against the ground.

"Attention!" Sharkie raises his arms, his ragged gray robes swaying in slow, ghostly motions. Beneath his huge hood, his eyes shine as two points of red light.

Sheila waves her eighteen-fingered hand in my direction. "Well, what'll your service be? Port-a-Potty Squad? Greeter at Ghoul-Mart?"

Pointing to Sharkie, I make a 'sh' face to Sheila. It's rude to talk once the ceremony starts, plus I hate answering the whole 'what'll your service be' question. Sheila nods and oozes away. Bonus.

THUD. THUD. THUD. THUD. Sharkie thumps his staff four more times. "I bring you the Oligarchy!"

Four ghouls in scarlet robes appear along the top tier of the stadium, one at each point of the compass. Called the Oligarchy, they rule Purgatory as one collective mind, and a not-so-creative mind too, based on how they name ghouls.

In one motion, the Oligarchy close their eyes, bow their gray heads, and open a series of massive portals around the lip of the stadium. Angels and demons appear in the dark openings, and then stream down the uneven stone steps in one great wave.

The angels take their seats in an orderly line, their bodies coming in many shapes, sizes and colors. All have massive white wings, floor-length linen robes, little open-toed sandals, and eyes that glow with an unearthly blue light. They can hide their wings if they want to, but they keep them out for important occasions, like watching Arena fights.

In other words, angels are cool.

On the other side of the stadium, the demons move in a frenzied pack, roaring in a mad rush for the best seats. Large, furry creatures stomp along next to small and slimy monsters. Tiny, spiked demons zoom above their heads. Eye color is all they share in common: black stands for 'neutral' while red means 'run for the hills.'

As I watch them scramble over each other, my head shakes from side to side. Demons are cool too, but only when I get to kill them.

The lively hum of stadium chatter collapses into anxious silence.

She is coming.

I scan the top level of the Arena. The four great portals stand empty and dark. Acting in unison, the Oligarchy ghouls lower their heads. A low hum fills the air. Pale yellow light glimmers in the eastern portal; all eyes turn in that direction. A figure in white appears in the darkened entryway. My breath catches.

This is Verus, Queen of the Angels.

She stands willowy and tall with long black hair, high cheekbones, and exotic, almond-shaped eyes. She's timeless, beautiful, and more than a little bit frightening. Sometimes she watches me so carefully during matches, it gives me the creeps.

Beside her stands a short-ish ghoul with a handsome face, square jaw, and large black eyes.

I elbow Walker in the ribs. "That guy could be your brother."

He looks up, smiles. "You don't say."

"I did say." I glance at him out of my right eye. "So, is he?"

"You know your mother doesn't allow me to share personal information." He shoots me a sympathetic smile. "Take it up with her later." He clears his throat and rocks a bit on his heels. "When I'm not around, if you don't mind."

My 'why don't you tell me anything' fights with Mom are nothing short of legend. I stick out my tongue at Walker. "Fine. I will."

Verus steps onto her balcony, a small entourage behind her. As she slips into a white stone throne, the stadium's silence is ripped apart by howls and screeches. A new outline appears in the western portal: Armageddon, the King of Hell. He's tall and lanky with black onyx skin that's smooth as polished stone. A blade-like nose divides his long face, ending in a pointed chin. He scans the stadium, his eyes blazing as two searing points of scarlet light. A shiny black tuxedo hugs his wiry frame.

Unholy Hell. Every nerve ending in my body goes on alert. While Verus is a wee bit scary, Armageddon gives off a 'greater demon' aura. If you get too close (which has happened to me more than once), every cell in your body shudders with terror. But that's not what *really* gets me about the King of Hell. Most demons are short-term thinkers. They want to kill your body and eat your soul, end of story. Not Armageddon. He planned for years to take over both Hell and Purgatory. That kind of craftiness brings evil to a new level.

Armageddon saunters away from the portal, a large entourage of gorilla-like Manus demons behind him. The Oligarchy collapse onto their knees as he passes by, their movements reminding me of marionettes whose strings are cut. Their deep voices echo through the stadium. "We praise thee, Great King." The ghouls may rule us in name, but everyone knows who *really* runs the show.

Without so much as a glance toward the Oligarchy, Armageddon speeds onto the balcony across from Verus, his entourage close behind him. The King of Hell slips into his own black stone throne.

Sharkie thumps his staff again. "Ghouls, demons, and angels!" The stadium falls silent.

I glance at my watch and grin. Right now, I should be in homeroom.

With a flourish of his bony arm, Sharkie gestures to the four scarlet-robed ghouls standing along the stadium's top level. "Today, the Oligarchy bring you a spectacle of governing efficiency: an Arena battle to the death witnessed by the magnificent leader of our joint troops in the Ghoul Wars… The acclaimed liberator of all Purgatory…Armageddon!"

The demons positively lose their freaking minds in a deafening cheer. My upper lip twists. *Screw Armageddon and his fake liberation of Purgatory. He handed us over to ghouls so we'd send more souls to Hell, pure and simple.* It's only when demon DNA mixes with a human that you get different powers. On their own, demons are mindless soul-munchers. My eyes flare red. I start to make a lewd hand gesture in Armageddon's direction, but Walker snags my wrist before I get too far. He shoots me a stern look, mouthing the words 'put a lid on it, Lewis.'

Nodding, I grip my hands behind my back. I'm enough of a warrior to know he's right: taunting Armageddon is a B-A-D idea. I focus on the ground, force myself to breathe slowly, and try to keep my cool. My inner demon has a mind of its own with more than my tail. When my eyes flare red, it's my demonic side getting rowdy. Sometimes, it's a struggle to keep it in check.

From his great stone throne, Armageddon watches the frenzied demon crowd, his thin red lips curling upwards. He scans every face, soaking in each expression and nuance, weaving them all into some complex and dark plan.

I shiver. He's being crafty again, and damn, that makes my skin crawl.

Raising his hand, Armageddon quiets the crowd. "Today's soul was a favorite of mine on earth. Unbelievable strength. No capacity for conscience. Pure untainted evil. When he wins this battle—which he will, make no mistake—then we'll finally have one of our own inside the gates of Heaven." The dark seats howl with glee while the angels collectively shiver. Grinning, Armageddon retakes his seat.

All faces turn to the Angel Verus. She slowly rises to her feet, her white wings spreading regally behind her. She shouts one word: "NEVER!" The force of her yell sets columns rattling and rubble tumbling to the ground. Her gaze turns to me, eyes flashing bright. Armageddon follows suit, his irises glowing red as he scans me from head to toe. A satisfied smirk winds the corner of his mouth. I've seen that look on other faces; it's the one that says 'that little girl? Maybe she's won before, but against this opponent? Are you serious?'

Which pisses me off, big time.

Sharkie thumps his staff again; a human soul appears nearby. In life, this ghost was a man about six feet tall with broad shoulders and two-hundred fifty pounds of solid muscle beneath them. Now he appears as a spectral version of his mortal self: a ghostly hulk whose pale body looks ready to burst from his faded jeans and dirty white t-shirt.

Sharkie addresses the spirit. "Vincent Francis Morris, you've chosen trial by combat, is this true?"

"The Choker. My name's...The Choker." Squinting his piggish eyes, the ghost flicks a fat tongue over his full lips.

"I will ask again." Sharkie's irises flare bright red. "Have you chosen trial by combat?"

The ghost curls his hands into fists. "Yes, combat."

"Select your opponent." Sharkie grins, his knife-like teeth glimmer in the pale light. "First, we offer XP-22."

The Choker eyes our 'fighting ghoul.' With barely-there skin and the muscle tone of toilet paper, anyone could crush XP-22. In fact, the Choker would probably snap him in three seconds or less, but I don't think he'll choose to. Ghouls look mighty terrifying, even the weak ones. Most humans avoid them.

The Choker is no different. "I'll pass."

Sharkie moves his thin arm to the next figure in line. "Second, we offer Sheila, the Limus demon."

Sheila's fourteen red eyes whip about her upper body, finally stopping to glare at the ghostly human. She stretches wide the black hole that serves as her mouth, letting out a gurgling roar. When that girl puts her game on, she's terrifying.

"Hmm." The Choker's beady eyes give Sheila a long stare; the entire Arena seems to hold its breath.

I glance at Sheila and shake my head. Limus demons are almost as easy to kill as XP-22. The trick is, they're super-flammable. One match and you turn a six-foot monster into a puddle of harmless goo. But like XP-22, they look worse than they actually fight.

The Choker frowns. "Nope."

"And third, we offer the quasi-demon, Myla."

The Choker's eyes slowly scan me from head to toe, his creepy gaze lingering on the curves under my t-shirt and sweats. Rage shoots up my spine. What a scumbag. If he stopped thinking with his pants for two seconds, he'd notice my demon tail instead of my boobs and butt. Some quasis get stuck with pig- or bunny-bottoms, but I hit the jackpot: the long and thin variety with an arrowhead end. Even better, it's coated in dragon scales, so the thing's nearly impossible to block or cut.

But the Choker isn't being smart. He stares into my big watery brown eyes and long lashes; I shamelessly blink in fake-terror. For trial by combat to be valid, the soul must have a chance at winning. They get three options, two of which are relatively easy to defeat. Then, there's me, the one nobody should pick. Except they always do.

"I choose her." His thick mouth stretches into a vicious smile. "I'll fight Myla." In a low voice, he adds: "You'll find out why they call me the Choker."

I jam my hands in my pockets and fake-shiver. *And you'll find out why they called me to fight you, dickhead.*

Sharkie thumps his staff on the ground again, and the ghostly Choker turns into two-hundred fifty pounds of real human. "So be it."

∼

End of Sample

Order ANGELBOUND today!

STANDARD APPENDIX OF
COOL STUFF

IF YOU ENJOYED THIS BOOK...

...Please consider leaving a review, even if it's just a line or two. Every bit truly helps, especially for those of us who don't *write by the numbers,* if you know what I mean.

Plus I have it on good authority that every time you review an indie author, somewhere an angel gets a mocha latte. For reals.

And angels need their caffeine, too.

COLLECTED WORKS

Fairy Tales of the Magicorum

Modern fairy tales with sass, action, and romance

1. Wolves and Roses
2. Moonlight and Midtown
3. Shifters and Glyphs
4. Slippers and Thieves
5. Bandits and Ball Gowns
6. Fire and Cinder
7. Fairies and Frosting
8. Towers and Tithes
9. Evil Queens and Goblin Kings

Angelbound Origins

About a quasi (part demon and part human) girl who loves kicking butt in Purgatory's Arena

1. Angelbound
2. Scala
3. Acca
4. Thrax

5. The Dark Lands
6. The Brutal Time
7. Armageddon
8. Quasi Redux
9. Clockwork Igni
10. Lady Reaper
11. Angry Gods
12. Phantom Corsair

Angelbound Lincoln

The Angelbound experience as told by Prince Lincoln

1. Duty Bound
2. Lincoln
3. Trickster
4. Baculum
5. Angelfire
6. Rixa
7. Mordred

Angelbound Offspring

The next generation takes on Heaven, Hell, and everything in between

1. Maxon
2. Portia
3. Zinnia
4. Rhodes
5. Kaps
6. Mack
7. Huntress

* *This is a completed series.*

Angelbound Xavier

Xavier's story

1. Archenemy
2. Archnemesis
3. Archangel

Pixieland Diaries

Sassy pixie Calla loves elf prince Dare. Too bad he hasn't noticed her. Yet.

1. Pixieland Diaries
2. Calla
3. Dare
4. Winter Prince
5. Ley Queen

Dimension Drift

Dystopian adventures with science, snark, and hot aliens

1. Scythe
2. Umbra
3. Alien Minds
4. ECHO Academy
This is a completed series.

Beholder

Where a medieval farm girl discovers necromancy and true love

1. Cursed
2. Concealed
3. Cherished
4. Crowned
5. Cradled
This is a completed series.

ACKNOWLEDGMENTS

If you're reading my freaking acknowledgements, chances are, I should thank you for something. So, for the record: you are awesome, dear reader.

That said, huge and heartfelt thanks must go out to my husband and son for their rock-solid support. Being an author means a lot of early mornings, late nights, long weekends, and never-ending patience. You two are the best guys in the universe, period.

After that, I must thank the extensive network of reviewers, friends and colleagues who helped me build my writing chops in general. Gracias.

Finally, deep affection goes out to my late, much loved, and dearly missed Aunt Sandy and Uncle Henry. You saw the writer in me, always. Thank you, first and last.

ABOUT CHRISTINA BAUER

Christina Bauer thinks that fantasy books are like bacon: they just make life better. All of which is why she writes romance novels that feature demons, dragons, wizards, witches, elves, elementals, and a bunch of random stuff that she brainstorms while riding the Boston T. Oh, and she includes lots of humor and kick-ass chicks, too. Christina lives in Newton, MA with her husband, son, and semi-insane golden retriever, Ruby.

Stalk Christina on Social Media

Blog:
http://monsterhousebooks.com/blog/category/christina

Facebook:
https://www.facebook.com/authorBauer/

Instagram:
https://www.instagram.com/christina_cb_bauer/

Twitter:
@CB_Bauer

VLOG:
https://tinyurl.com/Vlogbauer

Web site:
www.bauersbooks.com

COMPLIMENTARY BOOK

Get a FREE novella when you sign up for Christina's newsletter: https://tinyurl.com/bauersbooks

EXTRA APPENDIX THAT TAKES THE FIRST ONE AND KICKS ITS ASS

Q&A ON FIRE AND CINDER

ere are some questions I've been asked—and answers I've given—on my writing in general and FIRE AND CINDER specifically...

This novel is a fairy tale retelling. Why do you think fairy tales are still so popular?

Our brains are wired to enjoy the fairy tale storytelling space as somewhere safe to play around with different ideas and life paths. It meets a different and more primal need than reality-based stuff.

Who's your favorite character in FIRE AND CINDER?

Oh, that's tough to pick! It was really fun to write the character of Agatha. She's stuck as the *evil stepsister template* to

Elle's Cinderella... and in this book, Agatha gets her world turned on its ass. It was super fun to watch her grow!

What's your secret to write so many books, in different worlds, so fast? How do you balance it all?

Short answer: I have no idea.

Long answer: I'm probably on the autism spectrum. i've never had a formal diagnosis, but I did learn to camouflage my differences at a young age.

What's your favorite childhood memory involving books?

I used to sit in the doorway of my bedroom and read until I got caught by my parents and told to go back to sleep. Didn't occur to me to hide a flashlight under the comforter.

What fantastical fictional world would you want to live in (if any) given the chance?

I love *Lord of the Rings*, so it would be cool to retire in Rivendell. Elves know how to live the sweet life. True fact: I'd have chosen Lothlorien, but I'm afraid of heights.

What book do you feel is under-appreciated? How about overrated?

I think Edith Hamilton's MYTHOLOGY is an unknown classic. It really brings Greco-Roman myth to life... and those stories form the basis of so many great tales. For over-rated stuff, I make a conscious choice to keep those to myself. It's bad karma to dump on other author's work.

When you write a series, do you have an ending mapped out, or are you going through the journey at the same time as your characters?

Honestly, I keep thinking the next book will always be the last. After all, most series focus on a couple falling love. You can do a 'monster of the week' thing to keep it going, but I also try to find a new emotional arc, too. And just when I think it's over... BAM, another idea hits me!

Long story short? Yes, I am taking the journey at the same time as my characters!

How did you come up with your own fantasy world to write about? What is that process like for you to create your own kingdom?

It's really labor intensive. I create back stories and inspiration boards for all aspects of a world. But once it's all built, it feels like I'm just taking dictation. That's a rush that I adore!

That's all for now! Thanks for reading!

TOP 10 ADVICE FOR ASPIRING WRITERS

I'm often asked to share writing tips and tricks. Here's some classic advice for new authors!

Number Ten

Read a lot. Good stuff, bad crap, titles that make you giggle.

Number Nine

That said, be careful. For me, I take care not to read the same things as everyone else. I don't want to pick up plot points or whatever that are super popular and regurgitate them without knowing it. What you put in your head comes out on the page!

Number Eight

(Try to) accept critiques as a gift. After you cuss out your computer.

Number Seven

Decide if you want to self-pub based on what's best for you, not on what society says is cool.

Number Six

When people tell you that it's impossible to make money as an author, tell them that I said to pound salt.

Number Five

Write what you love. That way, if you're successful, you won't hate your life.

Number Four

Find joy in playing with language.

Number Three

Set aside a sacred time and place to write.

Number Two

Know that I believe in you.

Number One

Always remember: the stories in your heart can only be brought into the world by you. Please share them!

TIPS & TRICKS FOR WORLD BUILDING

*H*ere are three of my favorite tips and tricks for world building...

Tip #1... Pick a language base for the groups of people in your world

OK, so I got this one from Tolkien. He used the language and history of Finland in order to inspire his version of elves. In my experience, language drives so much of a character, it isn't even funny. It gives you a way to name them, the places in their lives and their history.

    PRO TIP: Google Translate is awesome here. There are also about a million web sites for baby names by culture.

Tip #2... Make Pinterest boards for key characters and places

I'm a super visual writer, so I start creating characters by building boards of inspirational pics. I begin with a general idea, such as the fact that the person is a ruler or whatever. Then I pull images onto my board. This takes time because I toss the stuff that doesn't fit and keep the pieces that do. In general, I delete about ten images for every one that works.

For me, it's also important to have a general Pinterest board of cool stuff that inspires me in general. I keep those boards hidden from general viewing. My public boards are here. Sarah J Maas has some cool boards that you may want to check out as well.

PRO TIP: Visit Pinterest if you haven't already.

Tip #3... Use a writing tool like Scrivener

This software allows me to organize research, move chapters around easily, and in general be a badass. You won't realize how much you've been craving it until you give it a try. I put all my 'world bibles' (lists of names, places and descriptions) in here, too.

PRO TIP: Check out Scrivener here.

So that's it... some of my favorite tools and tricks. Hope you found them helpful!

THAT TIME I DROVE INTO A GRAVEYARD AND KNOCKED OVER A TOMBSTONE

*T*his is such a random memory.

Still, I can't help but share it.

The year is 1986. I am a junior in high school and the family kid-mobile is a Chevy "Country Squire" station wagon. I'm talking the vehicular hotness of an automobile with fake wood paneling. Oh, yeah.

As the so-called kid car, the Country Squire was a nasty mess. The floor was filled with old McDonalds wrappers and used napkins. Strange food stains covered the seats. The alignment was so far off that to drive straight, you had to keep the steering wheel a quarter-turn to the right.

One day, I'm tooling down the highway and multi-tasking. In this case, I'm smoking and driving at the same time. At this point in my life, I attend Catholic school and see Marlboro Lights as a major form of rebellion. That said, I also keep the windows open so the stench of my sin will not soak into the car.

I turn off the main road. As I do so, I hardly notice the

graveyard to my right. Badass that I am, I toss my smoke out the window. It falls between the seat and the driver's side door.

Right onto an old napkin.

In my mind, this is about to blow up into a conflagration of epic proportions. I let go of the wheel, scoop up the napkin-n-smoke combo, and then chuck both out the window.

My first thought was, *whew.*

This was quickly followed by, *FUUUUUUUUCK!!!*

Sadly, letting go of the steering wheel is the equivalent of making a hard right.

Into the graveyard.

I knocked over two trees, a fence, and the tombstone of one Rosa Friedman, who died in 1898. I was unhurt, Rosa was already dead, and the Country Squire was trashed.

And that was how I drove into a graveyard and knocked over a tombstone.

-The End-